WITHDRAWN
PUBLIC LIBRARY
BROOKLINE

Winner Bakes All

The Cupcake Club

D0067385

Winner Bakes All

The Cupcake Club

Sheryl Berk and Carrie Berk

BROOKLINE PUBLIC LIBRARY

sourcebooks
jabberwocky

Putterham

3 1712 01423 9530

Copyright © 2013 by Sheryl Berk and Carrie Berk
Cover and internal design © 2013 by Sourcebooks, Inc.
Cover design by Rose Audette
Cover illustration © Julia Denos

Sourcebooks and the colophon are registered trademarks of Sourcebooks, Inc.

All rights reserved. No part of this book may be reproduced in any form or by
any electronic or mechanical means including information storage and retrieval
systems—except in the case of brief quotations embodied in critical articles or
reviews—without permission in writing from its publisher, Sourcebooks, Inc.

The characters and events portrayed in this book are fictitious or are used ficti-
tiously. Any similarity to real persons, living or dead, is purely coincidental and
not intended by the author.

Published by Sourcebooks Jabberwocky, an imprint of Sourcebooks, Inc.
P.O. Box 4410, Naperville, Illinois 60567-4410
(630) 961-3900
Fax: (630) 961-2168
www.jabberwockykids.com

Library of Congress Cataloging-in-Publication data is on file with the publisher.

Source of Production: Versa Press, East Peoria, Illinois, USA
Date of Production: December 2012
Run Number: 19418

Printed and bound in the United States of America.
VP 10 9 8 7 6 5 4 3 2 1

To Elizabeth Maria Walsh:
you are the meaning of champion.
Love,
Care Bear

Trouble Times Two

Sadie Harris kicked back on her bed, stretching her long legs up against the wooden headboard. She pitched a pink rubber ball against the wall, catching it effortlessly in her baseball glove, over and over.

"Quit the bouncing," her big brother Tyler shouted. His bedroom was on the other side. "I'm trying to study."

Sadie sighed. She needed to study, too. But she'd been wrestling with her math homework for more than an hour and it just refused to click.

She sat up and flipped open her math notebook. There it was, the still unsolved story problem: "Ms. Erikka had 420 pencils and 112 erasers. She kept 15 pencils and 5 erasers for herself, and now she needs to divide the rest evenly among 30 students. Write an equation and solve."

She stared at the question and it stared back at her, daring her to start writing. She had no clue where to begin. *Why does Ms. Erikka have so many pencils and erasers? And honestly, couldn't each student just take one and leave the extras in the supply basket? Did they have to make things so complicated?*

Sadie hated math. She hated it more than getting a cavity filled at the dentist. She hated it more than missing a jump shot in a basketball game. She couldn't explain it, but math made her feel all topsy-turvy inside. The bigger the equation, the more she panicked—and in fifth grade, the equations were *humongous*! As if that wasn't bad enough, her dyslexia often flipped the numbers around, so she had to really concentrate and check her answers two or three times to make sure she hadn't misread the numbers in the problem.

Her teacher, Ms. Erikka, was very patient with her. She gave Sadie extra time on tests and worked with her privately after class. But nothing seemed to help. "Math-phobia" is what Tyler called it. He had it in fifth grade, too.

"I couldn't add two plus two," he said, illustrating his point with four chocolate-chip cookies plucked out of the jar onto the kitchen counter.

"So how did you learn?" Sadie asked.

"I'm not sure," he replied. "One day in high school, we started learning geometry, and it all made sense to me. Like magic or something."

"Or something." Sadie chuckled.

"No, I'm serious. It was like someone flipped a switch in my brain and the numbers all made sense!"

Sadie nodded. It sounded crazy, but Ty had gotten a 97 on his last calculus test. She could see it tacked to the fridge with big red letters scribbled on top of the sheet that read, "Good job!"

Sadie doubted her math tests would ever have those happy red letters on them.

"You'll see," her mom assured her. "One day you'll just get it and you'll love math."

Love math? She seriously doubted it. There were things she was definitely good at, and math wasn't one of them. Sink a jump shot from the foul line…not a prob! Hit a home run with the bases loaded…piece of cake.

She'd even become an expert at baking, thanks to the cupcake club she and her friends Kylie Carson, Jenna Medina, and Lexi Poole had started the year before in fourth grade. In the beginning, she could barely read a recipe. Now she knew how to whip up a chocolate ganache from scratch and what the difference was between baking powder and baking soda.

"Some people are just born geniuses," her brother Corey

bragged. Sadie had to admit things did come fairly easily to
him. Not only had he been the captain of his middle school
basketball team, but now—in just the first few weeks of
high school—he had managed to land a spot on the foot-
ball squad.

"When ya got it…ya got it," Corey teased. "And I got
it big-time!"

"Yeah, and that matches those big feet!" Tyler coun-
tered, pointing to Corey's size 13EEE high-tops.

"Shaquille O'Neal wears a size twenty-two shoe,"
Corey replied.

"Does that mean you have more growing to do?" Mrs.
Harris sighed. "I just bought you new Nikes!"

Sadie giggled. Her brothers reminded her of one of
those old-time comedy duos—Laurel and Hardy or Abbott
and Costello. Or maybe even Phineas and Ferb? They were
always trying to one-up each other. But if there was one
thing *she* topped both of her brothers at, it was height.

At ten years old, she stood five feet, five inches tall—head
and shoulders above her classmates at Blakely Elementary.
When Corey and Tyler were her age, they barely measured
five feet. Sadie loved to look at the lines the Harris siblings
had made on the basement wall, marking their height at

every birthday. She was clearly the height champion for her age.

"You just sprung up like a beanstalk!" her mom told her. "Your brothers didn't have their growth spurts 'til middle school."

"But look at us now!" Tyler pointed out. "I'm six feet, two inches!"

"I hope Sadie doesn't get taller than that!" her mom fretted. "We'll need higher ceilings!"

Some of the kids at Blakely teased her about being so tall. Meredith Mitchell (Blakely's resident bully) loved to call her "Big Foot" and "Gigantua."

"How's the weather up there?" Meredith taunted her when they lined up to go to recess. Jack Yu cracked up: "Yeah, Sadie always has her head in the clouds!"

"Doesn't that bother you?" Kylie once asked her.

"Nope. I just think of Meredith as this teeny, tiny mosquito," Sadie told her. "Buzz…buzz…SPLAT!" She swatted the air and made Kylie crack up. "Besides, I kick her butt every time we're in P.E. She's all mouth…no game."

Even her coach had a "tall" nickname for Sadie: "Hey, Stretch! Let me see that defense!" The fact that people noticed her height never bothered Sadie. She was proud to be "Stretch Harris." Her brothers were tall. Her mom and dad were tall. In fact, almost everyone in the Harris family had the tall gene.

"Your grandpa Willie was six feet, five inches," her mother told her. "He would bump his head whenever he came through our door."

Sadie remembered her Papa Willie as a kind, gentle man, and she loved to look up to him when she was a little girl. It never bothered him if he had to duck while getting out of a car, and it never bothered her if she had to hug her knees when she sat in a crowded row in the movies.

But algebra was another story. *That* bothered Sadie big-time! Especially when Ms. Erikka called on her in class.

"Sadie, if 2 times n equals 96, what is n?" her teacher asked.

Sadie stared at the SMART Board, hoping for a number to magically materialize. No such luck. Couldn't she have a fairy godmother with a Magic Marker wand to give her a hint?

"Um…uh…I don't know," Sadie sighed.

"Well, take a guess!" Ms. Erikka encouraged her.

"Um, 18? 24? 36?" The class erupted in giggles.

"Can you tell us how you got those answers?" her teacher asked.

"Well, you told me to guess…" Sadie replied.

"A mathematical guess," Ms. Erikka corrected her. "One that's based on mathematical reasoning. Like what number doubled would give you 96?"

Sadie was still stumped. She had no idea what her teacher was talking about.

"Ooh, ooh! I know! It's 48!" Meredith waved her hand wildly in the air.

"No calling out, but, yes, thank you, Meredith, the answer is 48. Sadie, do you see how we got that?"

Sadie smiled and nodded, but what she was really thinking was, "I have no idea!"

She also had no clue how to solve this math homework problem about the pencils and erasers. She flopped back down on her bed and buried her head in her basketball pillow. If she failed math, the coach would kick her off the Blakely Bears. His rule was simple: no pass, no play.

Her teammates would never forgive her because she was the best chance they had for making the state championships this year. They knew it, and she knew it, so why wouldn't her brain cooperate? Why couldn't she just make those multiplication and division tables stick?

Suddenly, her cell phone rang and she dove for it on her desk. She recognized the number instantly. It was Kylie.

"What's the answer to question number 4?" she blurted out.

"What ever happened to 'Hey, girl? What's up?'" Kylie teased. "Is that how you talk to all the members of our cupcake club?"

"Nope…just the one who got a ninety-nine on the last math test. Seriously, Kylie, I'm stuck. I really need your help!"

"No sweat! I can come over—I wanted to try out a new recipe for white chocolate cupcakes anyway."

Her friend had a one-track brain, and it always led straight to cupcakes. That's why Kylie was president of their business, Peace, Love, and Cupcakes. She kept Sadie, Jenna, and Lexi up to their ears in flour and frosting every week.

"I dunno, Kylie," Sadie groaned. She glanced over at the dozens of trophies lined up on the shelf over her desk: basketball, track, soccer, softball. Her dad called it her "Wall of Fame." But the one prize she *really* wanted she hadn't won yet: the Elementary School Basketball State Championship cup. If it was up to Kylie, she'd have Sadie baking all afternoon—and they'd get so wrapped up in cupcakes that Sadie would forget all about her math quiz.

"I'll make you a deal," she bargained with Kylie. "You help me with my homework, and *then* we'll hit the mixer."

"Yay! I'll send Lexi and Jenna a text and tell them to come to your house," Kylie replied.

"I better make sure it's cool with my mom—hang on!" Sadie opened her bedroom door and shouted, "Hey, Mom! Is it okay if the cupcake club holds a taste test in our kitchen?"

She heard her mom's voice, but she couldn't make out what she was saying.

"What? I can't hear you!" Sadie called.

She climbed down a few steps on the staircase to get a better listen—and then realized her mom was talking to her dad, not to her.

"Ty needed new jeans, and Sadie's sneakers are too small! And Corey…well, he's growing out of everything…"

"You charged $300 on the Am Ex?" her father yelled. "We have to tighten the purse strings, Bria, not spend every cent we have on things we don't need."

"What would you like me to do, Gabe? Send your kids to school *barefoot?*"

Sadie gulped. They both sounded so angry at each other. She tiptoed back to her room and picked up her phone.

"I don't know if it's a good time," she told Kylie.

"What do you mean? It's always a good time to bake cupcakes!" Kylie insisted.

"It's just my parents…they're having a fight."

"Oh," Kylie said softly. "What about?"

"Money, I guess," Sadie sighed. "My dad's contracting business is pretty slow. He says it's because the economy is bad right now. No one is building or redecorating, so he doesn't have much work."

"Well, do you want to come over here instead?" Kylie offered.

Through her open door, Sadie could still hear her parents arguing. Getting out of the house sounded really good at the moment. She hated to think of her mom and dad fighting. But it was happening more and more lately—and it made Sadie worry. Her mom and dad couldn't seem to speak to each other anymore without getting angry.

Last night's disagreement had been one of the worst, and there wasn't any arguing involved. Over dinner, her father had announced there was no money to go on a ski trip over winter break this year.

"Aw, you're kidding me!" Corey moaned. "We always go skiing in Colorado."

"Well, not this year. Sorry," her dad replied. Sadie

noticed that her mother was looking down at her dinner plate, not saying a word.

"Can't we go for just a few days?" Tyler whined. "I was really looking forward to skiing the back bowls this year."

"This discussion is over," her dad snapped. "Next year."

"So what will we do over winter break?" Sadie asked. She knew most of her friends would be away for the holidays. Kylie's parents were taking her to Florida to visit her cousins, and Lexi had tickets to see the Radio City Christmas show with her Aunt Dee in New York.

"I was thinking you could visit Gram and Pops in Poughkeepsie," her dad said.

"*Poughkeepsie?*" Corey gasped. "What the heck do you do in Poughkeepsie for a week?"

Her mom finally spoke up. "There are some lovely museums."

Tyler made a face. "Yeah, that sounds like a whole lotta fun…"

"Pops is like a hundred years old," Corey groaned. "He only wants to watch old kung fu movies on TV. They don't even speak English in them. It's torture!"

"Hah-*yah*!" Sadie giggled, pretending to karate-chop her brother.

Just then, her mother rose from the table, slamming her plate into the sink. She was just as disappointed as they were. Sadie could feel it.

"I don't want to cancel our trip, but I have no choice," her dad tried to explain. "The airfare, the hotel, the meals, the ski rentals. How could we possibly afford it?"

Her mom stormed out of the kitchen and refused to say another word to her father all night. "The silent treatment" was what Tyler called it. "It's when she's super mad, so mad she can't even talk," he whispered. "This is *baaad*."

It was bad. Very bad. And Sadie didn't know how to explain all of this to Kylie. Her mom and dad argued once in a while—usually over silly things, like who forgot to close the garage door. It was nothing like this.

"Kylie, do you think my parents will get divorced?" Sadie asked softly. She knew her friend would give her a straight answer.

"Um, I don't know, Sadie. How bad are they fighting?"

Sadie filled Kylie in on yesterday's and today's fireworks.

There was silence on the other end of the phone. Sadie knew Kylie was thinking hard before she gave an answer.

"Well, lots of kids at Blakely Elementary have divorced

parents," she finally replied. Sadie thought that was her nice way of saying, "Yeah, it's a definite possibility."

"But I don't want mine to be divorced. It's awful! You live in two houses and have two rooms. You're always going back and forth…"

"Hey, don't frost the cupcake before it's cooled!" Kylie interrupted.

Sadie scratched her head. "What does that mean?"

"It means 'Don't think too fast.' Your parents haven't told you they're getting divorced!"

Sadie shook the ugly idea of divorce out of her head and tried to focus instead on happier thoughts—like spending the afternoon with the cupcake club and finishing her math homework in time to watch the Giants game on TV tonight. "Okay, I'll come over."

"Awesome!" Kylie cheered. Then she added gently, "Whatever happens, Sadie, you know we're all here for you, right?"

Sadie *did* know Kylie, Jenna, and Lexi would always stand by her. She remembered the time last year when she sprained her ankle and was on crutches for two weeks. She thought it was the end of the world, but the girls assured her it was only a temporary setback. She'd be back in the game in no time.

"It's like in *The Mummy Returns*," Kylie explained. "They think the mummy is gone for good…but no! He wakes up again to terrorize Brendan Fraser!"

Sadie rolled her eyes. "This is basketball, Kylie, not a monster movie."

"Kylie has a point," Lexi insisted. "The doctor said you'd be fine in two weeks."

"Two weeks!" Sadie moaned, gently touching her bandaged ankle. "I have to walk around on crutches! How am I supposed to go up and down the stairs at school?"

"Piggyback ride?" Jenna joked. "Or we could tie a rope around your waist and pull you up the side of the building through the science lab window…"

Sadie was moping for two days straight until the girls showed up at her doorstep with a plan to cheer her up.

"Cupcake delivery!" they announced when Mrs. Harris answered the door.

"Oh, my…come right in, girls. She's in the living room. Just be careful: she's not in a great mood and she bites!"

When Sadie turned around, she couldn't believe her eyes.

There were Kylie, Jenna, and Lexi, all dressed like giant cupcakes with silver foil wrappers around their hips and red "cherry" balloons tied to their heads. Each girl was wearing a white T-shirt "sprinkled" with multicolored specks of paint.

"Special delivery for Sadie Harris!" Jenna giggled. "A singing cupcake-gram!"

Kylie hit the Play button on her iPod touch, and hip-hop music filled the living room. The trio began to rap:

"Sadie, Sadie, don't be blue!
We've got a cupcake-gram for you!
What's tall and cool and super sweet?
Can you guess who'll be back on her feet?
Sadie, Sadie, give a cheer!
You'll get well soon, we have no fear!"

At the end of the rap, Kylie and Jenna got down on their hands and knees, and Lexi climbed on their backs, forming a pyramid. She wobbled but managed to stand up and toss confetti in the air. "Hugs and sprinkles from PLC!" all three shouted, showering the couch—and Sadie—with glittering shreds of paper.

Sadie and her mom applauded wildly. "That was amazing, girls," her mother said. "Love the costumes!"

Lexi climbed down. "Aren't they cool? It was my idea to do the cherries on top." She took off the balloon and handed it to Sadie. "At least we got you to smile!"

Sadie had to admit that she did feel better. They'd even baked her get-well cupcakes with cute little fondant crutches on top.

"This is really nice of you," she said, licking the chocolate buttercream off her fingers.

"You didn't think we'd let you sit around feeling sorry for yourself, did you?" Kylie asked. "If you can't come to the cupcakes, the cupcakes will come to you!"

Sadie would never forget how the girls had managed to take her mind off her troubles. But divorce wasn't as simple to fix as a sprained ankle. And no amount of cupcakes could help her pass fifth-grade math if she failed her quiz this week. What would she do? What *could* she do?

Kylie read her mind. "We'll work it out," she assured Sadie.

Let It Snow!

"We need to come up with a new cupcake of the month," Kylie told her fellow PLC-ers. "Something that's wintery." They had spread dozens of cookbooks on Kylie's bed and were flipping through the pages, searching for ideas.

"What about angel food cake...with snow angels on top?" Lexi suggested, holding up her notebook. Sadie checked out her sketch: it was beautifully drawn as always, and the cupcakes looked heavenly.

"I'm thinking candy cane cupcakes—with peppermint frosting," Jenna piped up. "Or what about hot cocoa cupcakes...with mini marshmallows? You know me...it's all about the flavor."

"I think those are all cool," Kylie agreed. "Especially with the forecast this week. They're predicting a major blizzard in the Northeast."

"Can you say, 'Snow Day'?" Jenna exclaimed. "I have

this awesome flying saucer sled. *Vamos a la nieve!* Let it snow!"

"Snowball fight!" Kylie chimed in. "You are so going down, Jenna!"

"I'm just hoping it hits before Friday's math quiz," Sadie added. "Don't you think they'll close school if we get a foot of snow?"

"Probably, and that will give us a chance to work on our designs," Lexi said, getting down to cupcake business. She grabbed her sketchbook and began drawing. "What if we sprinkled the top of a white chocolate cupcake with shredded coconut to look like a snowball?" She held up her sketch.

"Mr. Ludwig will love those for the Golden Spoon," Kylie said. "Snowball cupcakes in honor of the blizzard!" The girls knew their steady customer would want a brand-new batch of cupcakes to sell in his gourmet shop in Greenwich as soon as possible. He'd already left Kylie two messages asking when he could get his delivery this week.

He was a loyal friend to Peace, Love, and Cupcakes. After all, he'd given them their very first business contract after sampling one of their chocolate cupcakes at a school event. Thanks to Mr. Ludwig, they had become more than just a Blakely Elementary School cupcake club. They were now a real baking business. But he wasn't the most patient person on the planet!

"Maybe we should send out an email blast," Jenna pointed out. "Let our customers know we've got new flavors. It might help our business pick up a little…"

Kylie flipped through their accounting log. Jenna was right. They had been selling five or six dozen fewer every week. Even Mr. Ludwig had reduced his weekly order from 300 to 240 cupcakes, and just this past weekend they'd had a birthday order cancellation at the last minute.

"I think it's the economy," Sadie said. "My dad says things are tough all over."

Jenna nodded. "You can say that again."

"Is your family okay?" Sadie had almost forgotten that Ms. Medina was a single mom with five kids. Jenna's family didn't have a lot of money to begin with, and her mom relied heavily on her job in a tailor shop.

"My mom says people always need their clothes sewn and hemmed. The less new stuff you can afford to buy, the more you have to fix what you have. She and my two older sisters have been pretty busy lately."

Sadie was relieved. At least someone was doing well. She wished she could say the same for her family. She didn't dare tell her parents that her basketball coach had mentioned buying new team uniforms this year. They'd freak because the uniform would cost a fortune.

"Maybe your mom could get a job as a seamstress," Jenna suggested.

Sadie chuckled at the thought. Her mom couldn't even sew on a button. Last year, Sadie had torn her track shorts before a meet and asked her mom to sew them. Her mom had no idea what to do with a needle and thread, so she'd used a stapler and tape to repair the shorts. Just as Sadie crossed the finish line, she heard "*Rip!*" and felt a draft. She didn't realize what had happened until the track team captain pointed to her butt and giggled, "Nice polka-dot panties!"

"I don't think my mom is the sewing type," Sadie reflected.

"Well, what is she good at?" Lexi asked. "She must be good at something."

Sadie twirled her ponytail. "Well, she's good at being a mom. She always says it's the best job anyone could ever have."

"That's true," Lexi replied, "but it doesn't pay much, does it?"

"Maybe you could help. Do some baby-sitting on the side," Kylie offered.

Sadie already felt like she had three full-time jobs: the

cupcake club, the basketball team, and being a fifth-grader. She couldn't imagine piling more on her plate, but she felt like she needed to do something to help her family.

"We're just going to have to make more money with PLC," she told her friends. "I think the more money my family has, the less my parents will fight."

She noticed that Kylie had been awfully quiet this whole time—which usually meant she was cooking up a crazy cupcake plan.

"Kylie?" Sadie tapped her friend on the shoulder. "What are you thinking?"

"I got it!" Kylie spun around in her desk chair. "Peace, Love, and Cupcakes Points!"

Sadie raised an eyebrow. "Points? Points for what? Like a video game?"

"It's like the frequent-shopper cards my mom uses at the pharmacy and the grocery store," Kylie explained. "For every cupcake you buy, you collect points until you earn enough to get a dozen free. In our case, if you buy three dozen cupcakes in a month, you get one dozen free."

"That's a great idea, Kylie!" Lexi exclaimed. "People will order from us every week to earn their cupcake points. We'll have tons of orders!"

"And tons of deliveries to make," Jenna pointed out. "What do we do about that?"

"Tyler and Corey will help with the deliveries," Sadie volunteered. She knew she could convince them—especially if it helped make peace between their parents.

"Maybe we should paint Tyler's car to look like a cupcake-mobile," Lexi suggested. "Cupcake trucks are really popular in New York City. I saw a lot of them there when I was staying with Aunt Dee."

Sadie shook her head. "I don't think my brother would appreciate that. He thinks his Honda is a 'babe magnet.'" The girls all giggled.

"What should we say in the email subject line?" Kylie asked. She opened her laptop and began typing.

"What about 'Get to the point!'" Jenna joked. "As in PLC Points."

Sadie thought about what would get her attention in an email. "How about, 'Sweet Rewards: Free Cupcakes for PLC Customers!'"

"Love it!" Kylie high-fived her. "This is going to be our biggest selling week ever!"

3

A Storm Is Brewing

The next day at school, the girls needed to run their plan by Juliette Dubois, PLC's advisor and Blakely's drama teacher. Juliette was always very practical with her advice for their business—but she also encouraged them to think big.

"A points program makes a lot of sense," she said. "Everyone is looking for bargains right now. I've been clipping coupons trying to save money myself. And you'll learn a very important lesson: creating customer loyalty will mean long-term sales."

Kylie showed her their idea for the email blast.

"So how long do you intend to run this points program?" Juliette asked.

"We hadn't really thought about that," Sadie answered. "I guess we could run it for a month."

"I think you might need longer than that to get people

hooked," Juliette considered. "I'd say give it a try for three months and see how it does. When are you sending out the email blast—and to how many customers?"

Kylie gulped. "Wow. We didn't think about that either. I guess our entire customer list—that's 500 people. We could get it out tomorrow so people could order for the weekend."

"Now that's a plan, man!" Juliette cheered. "Go to it, girls!"

A day later, the club was flooded with requests for PLC's Cupcake of the Week: "There's No Business like Snow Business." The girls gathered at Sadie's house to bake, decorate, and box the orders so her brothers could deliver them.

"I am totally going to fail my math quiz Friday," Sadie sighed. "With all of this baking, how will I study?"

"We'll bake *and* study," Kylie insisted.

Jenna held up her hands, which were covered in flour and buttercream. "Um, I wouldn't bring any math textbooks in this kitchen at the moment. It's a mess!"

"You see?" Sadie said. "It's hopeless."

"Relax and focus on cupcake math," Kylie insisted.

Lexi giggled. "Now that would be a cool subject in school! Do you get to frost as you do your fractions?"

Kylie continued: "Sadie, we have a total of 216 cupcakes to bake and have four dozen already in the oven. How many do we have left to bake?"

Sadie thought hard and tried to picture the equation in her head. "Well, 4 times 12 equals 48," she began. "So 216 minus 48 would be 168."

Kylie applauded. "And how many dozen is that? Write an equation and solve!"

Sadie closed her eyes and saw cupcakes lined up on a countertop. She pictured them in groups of 12. The equation would be: 168 divided by 12 equals x. So x would be 14.

"We have 14 dozen left to go!" Sadie answered.

"*Muy bueno*!" Jenna cheered. "You are so going to pass that quiz Friday!"

A few flakes started falling outside the window just as the girls were putting the cupcakes in the oven. But by the time the last dozen were piped with white chocolate frosting and dipped in shredded coconut, the winds were whipping up and the ground was covered by a white blanket of snow.

"I thought they didn't say snow 'til Thursday night," Lexi said, peering outside.

"That's weathermen for you," Mrs. Harris sighed. "I guess they were off by a day." She looked concerned.

"Now your father is going to have to stop working on the Saperstones' garage door. It's getting bad out there quickly."

Kylie peered out the window. "I don't think I can bike home in this…"

Mrs. Harris nodded. "I think you should all call your parents and tell them you'll be sleeping over here tonight. We'll see how bad it is in the morning."

Kylie, Jenna, and Lexi cheered: "Slumber party!"

"Better not let my brothers hear that…" Sadie warned. She knew Corey and Tyler would be up to all sorts of tricks if they heard her friends were staying over.

But it was too late. "I smell something good…Hand it over!" Corey demanded. He bounded into the kitchen, tracking snow across the floor, and dropped his dripping wet jacket over the back of a chair.

"Say *please*," Mrs. Harris corrected him.

"Okay…*please* hand it over," Corey joked.

Jenna offered him a cupcake, and he inhaled it in two bites. "Would you like to know what you just ate?" she asked.

"Nope. Just give me another one…" He licked his lips. "Or I will torture you guys all night with practical jokes. Did I ever tell you about the itching powder I put in Sadie's sleeping bag when she was eight?"

The girls looked at Sadie for confirmation. "Give him another cupcake," she said. "I itched for days."

"I hope the snow doesn't shut down all the roads," Kylie suddenly thought. "How will we get all these cupcakes delivered?"

"Dogsled?" Corey teased, helping himself to a third cupcake. "Mush! Mush!"

"Nah…reindeer are better," called a voice from the living room. "On Donner, on Blitzen…" Sadie's brother Tyler appeared in the kitchen, covered in snow. "It's really coming down out there." He scooped a cupcake off the counter and popped it whole in his mouth.

Kylie, Jenna, and Lexi all stared.

"Don't look so surprised," Sadie teased. "My big brothers are human vacuum cleaners. They eat anything that's not nailed down."

Tyler swallowed and let out a huge burp. "Yes, siree, that's me!" He was starting to grab another cupcake when Mrs. Harris swatted his hand away.

"Enough, you two! You'll spoil your dinner. Go get changed and washed up. And girls, let's get this kitchen clean. I know there must be a table somewhere under all that shredded coconut."

Kylie grabbed a broom and helped Sadie sweep the floor. "So…your family seems okay?" she whispered.

Sadie shrugged. "I guess…for now."

☆ ☮ ☆

Sadie's father finally arrived home nearly two hours later. The roads were iced over, and his truck could barely make its way up the steep hill to their house.

"What a night!" he exclaimed as he opened the front door. His black mustache and beard were white with snow.

"Daddy!" Sadie raced to give him a hug. "I was getting worried!"

"What's that? A fraidy Sadie? I never heard of such a thing!" he teased.

Sadie shivered. "Your nose feels like a Popsicle!"

"I was out in the snow for over an hour trying to fix the Saperstones' garage door opener."

"Did you see Jeremy?" Lexi piped up, eager to hear news about her "boyfriend," the Saperstones' youngest son.

"You mean your Romeo?" Jenna teased, referring to the Shakespeare play, *Romeo and Juliet*, they had performed in drama class.

"Jeremy's snowed in just like you ladies," Mr. Harris

said. "Chess practice canceled or something like that." He brushed the snow off the bottoms of his jeans.

"Ooh! I'll go call him now!" Lexi squealed. Sadie rolled her eyes. She couldn't understand how Lexi could care so much about a boy. Sadie had a house full of them…and it was no big deal!

"Did you finish the Saperstones' door?" Mrs. Harris asked hopefully.

He shook his head. "No. I have to do more work on it when this storm blows over."

Sadie guessed that meant no pay for his work today. She tried to wipe the look of disappointment off his face.

"Eskimo kiss!" she said, rubbing noses. "With a real, live Eskimo!"

He smiled, but Sadie saw that her mom was frowning. "I'll reheat your dinner, Gabe," she said, and shuffled back to the kitchen.

Later that evening, Jenna and Lexi made themselves comfy in sleeping bags on the living-room rug while Kylie and Sadie shared the foldout couch. Sadie flipped channels until she found Connecticut's *Battle of the Bakers*. "I want the old lady from Beacon Falls to win tonight's battle," Jenna said, stuffing a handful of popcorn in her mouth. "Go, Granny Annie's Cupcakes!"

"How cool would it be to be on this show?" Kylie daydreamed. "We could totally win, you know. And the prize is $5,000!"

Lexi thought it over. "We might have a chance. But first you have to make an audition video and send it in."

"So let's make a video!" Kylie insisted. "We could do it tomorrow—I bet there'll be no school. Maybe not even Thursday or Friday."

"Uh, are you forgetting something? Our cupcake deliveries?" Sadie pointed to the boxes piled high on the dining-room table. "No deliveries, no money."

"I'm sure they'll plow the roads by midday, and your brothers will be able to drive them over," Lexi said.

"I need more popcorn for Round 2," Jenna said, waving the empty bowl. "Would ya mind, Sadie?"

Sadie took the bowl and was about to barge into the kitchen when the sound of low, angry voices stopped her. She put her ear against the door and heard her parents. They were at it again.

"I worked all day for nothing!" her father snapped.

"Well, that's not my fault!" her mother barked back.

Sadie couldn't stand it anymore. Why were they always bickering? Why couldn't they get along?

"Hey, Sadie…where's that popcorn? Commercial's over!" Jenna called.

Kylie was the one who noticed Sadie frozen at the kitchen door, clutching the bowl to her chest and eaves-dropping. "You okay, Sadie?" she called.

Just then, the tears welled in the corners of her eyes and Sadie couldn't stop them from spilling down her cheeks. She didn't want her friends to think she was a baby, but she couldn't help crying. She felt like her heart was break-ing in two.

"No, I'm not okay!" she sobbed, flinging the empty bowl to the floor. "My parents are getting a divorce!"

4

Lights, Camera, Cupcakes!

Sadie's friends tried to calm her down, but it was no use. She was inconsolable.

"I think you should talk to your parents and tell them how worried you are," Kylie told her.

No way! The last thing she needed tonight was more family drama. She was grateful when her mom went upstairs and slammed the door to her bedroom while her father retreated to his home office. Neither of them noticed how upset *she* was or suspected she had overheard.

"Even if your parents do split up, it'll be okay," Jenna insisted. "My mom does a great job raising us all by herself."

"I don't want my parents to split up," Sadie sniffled. "I want us to be the same happy family we were before!"

"Maybe you will be." Lexi put an arm around her. "Maybe things will get better."

"Or maybe they'll get worse…just like the snowstorm!" Sadie replied.

It was after midnight before she finally fell asleep. The girls were all joking and complaining about Jenna's loud snoring, but Sadie found it soothing—kind of like the sound of an electric mixer on low speed. At least it took her mind off her problems.

The next morning, the gray storm clouds rolled away to reveal a bright blue sky. Sadie woke up and rubbed her eyes. They felt sore and swollen from crying. She noticed that it was 10 a.m. and she was the only one still in bed. School was closed! The girls were already dressed and in the kitchen, making phone calls and trying to convince Tyler and Corey to drive their cupcakes around the neighborhood. She hoped everyone would be too busy to bring up last night. She wanted to pretend it never happened.

"My car will never make it in two feet of snow," Tyler replied, taking a swig of orange juice from a container in the fridge. "I don't even think Dad's truck could plow through that."

"You're gonna have to wait 'til the roads thaw out," Corey added. He was a freshman in high school and thought he knew everything.

"When will that be?" Kylie asked.

"Oh, I dunno. Maybe May or June?" He chuckled.

"Not funny," Sadie said, shuffling into the kitchen. "We have to get the cupcakes delivered."

Kylie nodded. "Your sis has spoken. Morning, Sadie!"

As Kylie had predicted, school was closed until the roads could reopen. "We're kinda trapped here for a few hours," Lexi filled her in. "Nothing can go out or come in."

"Which means we have the perfect opportunity to make a video for *Battle of the Bakers*," Kylie suggested. "We have it all planned out already—Jenna kept us up with her snoring!"

"I can't help it." Jenna shrugged. "My sister says I sound like a lawn mower."

Sadie interrupted: "Electric mixer, actually. Your snoring put me to sleep."

"Not me!" Lexi complained. "I tried putting the pillow over my head, even putting on my earphones, but she was just too loud!"

"At least we got some great video ideas cooked up!"

Kylie pointed out. She handed Corey her cell phone. "You can film us."

Corey protested: "Do I look like Steven Spielberg to you?"

Sadie smirked. "No prob, Core. I guess I'll just have to tell Mom how we got that big blue stain on the upstairs rug. Do I need to remind you about your science project accident? The blue Jell-O explosion?"

Her brother winced. "You wouldn't…"

"Wouldn't I?" Sadie batted her eyelashes. She might be the little sister, but she knew how to get her brothers to do what she wanted.

"Go, Sadie!" Kylie laughed. "She shoots! She scores!" She handed the phone to Corey and showed him how to hit Record.

"We're going to start off by introducing ourselves: who we are, and what makes Peace, Love, and Cupcakes so cool," Kylie suggested. She turned to Corey and gave him his cue. "*Action!*"

Tyler snickered. "What are you gonna call your video? The Real Cupcake Bakers of Connecticut? America's Got Cupcakes? Project Cupcakes?"

The girls ignored him. "Hi, I'm Kylie…I'm Jenna…I'm Lexi…I'm Sadie…"

Corey turned the camera to face himself. "And I'm Corey! My sister and her weird friends are shooting this dumb video…"

"Ignore him." Sadie frowned. "We can edit that out. Keep going, Kylie…"

"Together, we are Peace, Love, and Cupcakes—the best cupcake bakers in Connecticut! We're only in fifth grade, and we have our own cupcake business. Just look what we can do!"

She pointed to Lexi, who expertly piped a beautiful rose on top of a cupcake. "First I fill the bag, then I squeeze it like this," she instructed. "Just a little puff of pressure and you've got the perfect petal."

Next, Kylie signaled Sadie who cracked eggs one-handed. "The trick is to make one, firm tap on the bowl with the egg so it cracks cleanly," Sadie explained. "Not a shell in sight!"

Finally, Jenna whipped a flawless lavender buttercream in a mixer. "Always taste your frosting to make sure it's the perfect sweetness and texture," she said. She took a lick of frosting off her pinkie. "*Perfecto!*"

Then all three of them rolled fondant and stamped out the letters PLC and a peace sign and placed them on top of four cupcakes. They each held a cupcake up to the camera and shouted together, "PLC *rocks!*" With that, Tyler snuck up behind them and dumped a bag of flour over Sadie's head.

"Now that's a wrap!" Corey laughed, zooming in for a close-up.

Sadie was about to scream when her mom walked in to see what all the commotion was about.

"Clean it up," she said sternly. "And apologize to your sister. Both of you."

Sadie showered and changed and came back downstairs to see the final video Lexi had put together with iMovie on her laptop.

"It's so cool, Lex," Jenna exclaimed. "I love how you put in pics of our best cupcake creations—like the swaying palm tree we made out of mango mini cupcakes. And the giant Ferris wheel that spun rainbow tie-dyed cupcakes. We really look like professional bakers."

"We *are* professional bakers," Kylie insisted. "Which is why we're going to get picked for *Battle of the Bakers*. You'll see!"

Sadie wasn't as convinced, but she liked the sound track

Lexi had spliced in: Gwen Stefani's "The Sweet Escape." She doubted Granny Annie's audition sounded this cool!

"Maybe we can get Mr. Ludwig to say something on camera for us," Kylie added. "Something like, 'Their cupcakes are my best sellers!'"

Jenna groaned. "He'd probably say, 'I discovered them! I take all the credit!' But I guess it's worth a try."

Kylie dialed the number for the Golden Spoon. "That's strange," she said. "It says the number's out of service."

"Maybe the storm downed the phone lines in Greenwich," Mrs. Harris suggested. "The radio says the roads should be open in the next few hours, so maybe Sadie's dad can take you over there with your delivery."

By 3 p.m., the girls were able to pile into Mr. Harris's truck. They strapped the boxes of cupcakes to the flatbed and crossed their fingers that the truck wouldn't skid on the icy roads. Everyone was delighted that PLC was able to deliver—especially a five-year-old girl named Dale who'd been crying all morning.

"I thought my birthday was ruined," she whimpered. Sadie smiled and opened a box to reveal a dozen Rapunzel cupcakes, each with a long braid of orange licorice "hair" on top.

"I love them!" the birthday girl said, hugging Sadie tightly around the knees. "Thank you so, so much!"

"Did you get that for the video?" Sadie winked at Kylie. "Another happy PLC customer!"

Kylie checked her watch—it was nearly 4 p.m. And they'd promised Mr. Ludwig yesterday his delivery would be there by 8 a.m.!

"I don't think our next customer is going to be as happy," she warned. "Mr. Ludwig hates when we're late. And this time, we're super late and couldn't even reach him."

"Hop in, cupcakers," Mr. Harris called. "Next stop... the Golden Spoon."

Golden Opportunity

When Mr. Harris pulled up to the store, there was huge sign out front that read, "CLOSED FOR DISASTER."

"Disaster? What kind of disaster?" Kylie wondered out loud. She knocked on the front door. "Mr. Ludwig? Are you in there?"

"Go away!" said a meek voice. "Can't you read the sign?"

"But we brought you your order!" said Lexi.

"Didn't you hear me? I said GO!" the voice shouted.

"Let's go, girls," Mr. Harris said. "He obviously doesn't want any cupcakes."

"*Wait!*" Sadie shouted. "Mr. Ludwig! It's us, Peace, Love, and Cupcakes!"

The lock slowly turned and the door creaked open. There was Mr. Ludwig, bundled in his coat, hat, and scarf. Sadie thought he looked like she had this morning: all red-eyed and puffy. Had he been crying, too?

"What's wrong?" she asked. "You look awful!"

"What's wrong? Isn't it obvious?" he replied. "There's an enormous hole in my roof, and my entire store is buried under snow and water! I'm ruined!"

Mr. Harris surveyed the huge hole in the roof. "It gave under the weight of the snow," he said. "It's pretty bad but probably fixable." The glass display cases were shattered, all the shelving had fallen off the walls, and the floor was about a foot under water. Mr. Ludwig kept holding his head in his hands, moaning.

"Fixable? I've called everyone in the tristate area, begging them to fix it. No one can get my store open. They're saying it will take months. But to be closed for months— that would be end of the Golden Spoon for sure."

"Does this mean you don't want your 240 cupcakes?" Jenna asked.

Sadie elbowed her in the ribs. "We totally understand, Mr. Ludwig," she replied. "But I know someone who can fix it."

"You do? Who?" Mr. Ludwig's face brightened.

Sadie grabbed her dad's hand and pulled him forward. "Him. My dad. Harris Contracting. He's a great builder."

Mr. Harris looked shocked. "I, um, well, I…" he began.

"Thanks for the vote of confidence, honey, but I don't know if I can fix it."

"Of course you can!" Sadie insisted. "You can fix anything! Remember when PLC built that Statue of Liberty out of key lime cupcakes and her head kept falling off? You totally stuck it on with Gorilla Glue."

"Honey, that was a cupcake sculpture. This is a roof that's been totaled. I can't use Gorilla Glue. I don't even know where to begin."

"Please, Dad," Sadie pleaded. "I'm sure Mr. Ludwig would pay you to fix it fast."

"Oh, yes. If you can get it fixed in a few weeks and I can open my store, I would be so grateful!" Mr. Ludwig begged.

"Pretty please with frosting on top?" Sadie threw in. She knew that a quick paycheck was just what her dad needed—and that might put an end to all the arguing at home.

"I'll have to think about," Mr. Harris said. "I'll let you know tonight."

After Mr. Harris dropped Jenna, Lexi, and Kylie off at their homes, Sadie cranked up the car radio and stared out the window. Selena Gomez was singing "Falling Down," and that's exactly how she felt—like the world was falling down around her. She was furious at her father for blowing this "Golden" opportunity. What was wrong with him?

"I know you're angry," he said. Sadie pretended not to hear. "Ignoring me isn't helping."

"Well, you're not helping either!" she fired back. "You and Mom say we have no money. You're always fighting over it. Why wouldn't you take that job?"

"Because I don't make promises I can't keep," her father explained. "Would you take an order for 10,000 cupcakes in two hours if you knew it was impossible to deliver?"

"It's not the same thing," Sadie sniffed.

"No, it's not. Fixing a roof is a major job, honey. What Mr. Ludwig is asking may be impossible. We're not talking a little leak or a few broken shingles. We're talking a giant hole and major water damage. The Golden Spoon is totaled."

"But won't you just try?" Sadie insisted. "How do you know if it's impossible unless you try?"

"I said I'll think about it. I need to take some measurements and get some estimates on the materials."

At least, Sadie thought, he wasn't completely giving up. That was a relief! But she didn't feel much better when her mom told her the roads were open and school would be in session tomorrow. "Everything is back to normal," Mrs. Harris said.

Sadie wished that was true. She used to think her parents were so romantic and "mushy." They held hands at the movies and kissed each other hello and good-bye.

"When I met your father, it was like a bolt of lightning struck me," her mom had confided in her once. "He was handsome, strong, charming. He absolutely swept me off my feet."

What happened between them? Sadie wondered. She looked at their wedding picture on the mantel. Her mom wore an elegant, strapless, white lace gown and veil, and her dad was in a top hat and tails. They looked so in love! When had things started to fall apart?

Sadie suddenly remembered what her dad had told her on the car ride home: "Sometimes you can try and try, but something is just too broken to be fixed."

She gulped. Was he talking about the Golden Spoon's roof....or her parents' marriage? Was that too broken to fix as well? Had he and her mom decided they were done trying?

When Friday arrived, Sadie almost forgot about her pop quiz in math. She'd been so worried about her parents, and so angry over the Golden Spoon job, that she hadn't had time to panic over it. Ms. Erikka handed her the test sheet and smiled. "I know you can do it, Sadie," she said. "Just take your time, check your work, and *breathe*."

Sadie remembered how Kylie had told her to picture things instead of numbers. "Make the equation real to you," she'd advised. So when the question asked how many cars were needed to drive forty-five students on a class trip, Sadie pictured her dad driving her and her three friends to the Golden Spoon on Thursday. One driver and four people could fit in each car…that meant they would need nine cars. She got it!

"How do you think you did?" Kylie pulled her aside as the class bell rang.

"Okay," Sadie shrugged. "I'm pretty sure I passed."

"Yay!" Kylie hugged her. "And I have some more good news. Principal Fontina said we could set up a table in the cafeteria with the 240 cupcakes the Golden Spoon couldn't use and sell them—as long as we donated half the money to the Blakely Eco Center."

"Cool," Sadie replied. "So at least we'll make back some money to cover the cost of those ingredients."

"Now on to our next problem," Jenna said, sneaking up behind them in the hall. "What are we going to do without the Golden Spoon's weekly order?"

Sadie hadn't even considered the impact the Golden Spoon closing would have on PLC. Kylie was right: Mr. Ludwig was their biggest customer—and a steady paycheck. Without his business, they'd have to scale back for sure. And that was not what any of them wanted. PLC was going to be even bigger and better this year…they'd promised themselves!

"You have to convince your dad to repair the roof," Jenna said.

"I tried. He won't listen to me." Sadie sighed. "He says it's impossible. He's taking some measurements, but he's convinced it's not going to work."

"Nothing is impossible," Kylie insisted. "I used to think

having a cupcake club was impossible. You used to think learning math was impossible. We've proved everyone wrong, right?"

Sadie thought about it. She had to make her dad see things her way.

"I have an idea," she told Kylie and Jenna. "Meet me at the basketball game tonight—and bring Lexi! We need all the help we can get!"

When she got home, her father was at his desk in the den, crunching numbers on his calculator. He was surrounded by a stack of bills, and Sadie knew he was stressed out. So she treaded lightly.

"Hey, Dad, you coming to my basketball game tonight at the gym?" she asked.

Mr. Harris looked up, happy that Sadie was speaking to him. "Wouldn't miss it for the world, hon." He smiled.

"I hear the North Canaan Cougars are a tough team to beat."

"Not for my girl," Mr. Harris said. "You'll cream 'em," he added.

"So you're saying, *nothing* is impossible?"

Mr. Harris looked up from his desk. "What are you up to, Sadie?" he asked.

"Nothing!" Sadie planted a kiss on his cheek.

She raced upstairs to get into her uniform. At the game, she made sure that her PLC members were seated right behind her family on the bleachers. "I'm going to go for a long shot, and when I make it, I want you to make sure to remind my dad: 'Nothing is impossible.' Got that?"

Lexi looked puzzled. "Is that code for something?"

"Yes, it's code for 'Fix Mr. Ludwig's roof!'" Sadie explained. "Just make sure he gets it, okay?"

"Check that," Jenna teased. "Operation Convince Daddy is underway!"

"But, Sadie…what if you miss the shot?" Kylie asked.

"I won't. I can't," Sadie replied.

The Blakely Bears were trailing the North Canaan Cougars by one point with only two seconds left in the game. Sadie grabbed the ball and headed down the court. The Cougar defender on her was enormous—at least a head taller than Sadie—and she was waving her arms in the air, blocking Sadie no matter which way she turned. The girl had her completely boxed in.

"She'll never make it!" Lexi cried, covering her eyes. "I can't watch!"

"Go, Sadie!" her father cheered. "You can do it!"

Just then, Sadie faked out the Cougar player. She zigged while defense zagged.

"Go!" screamed her PLC mates. "Go, Sadie, go!"

She broke free and headed down court, straight for the net. But it was still a tough shot from far away.

"It's impossible to sink that," Kylie piped up. "Don't you think, Mr. Harris?"

Sadie threw the ball, and it landed with a swoosh through the hoop. The Bears won the game, and the team lifted Sadie on their shoulders and carried her down the court.

"Woo-hoo! That's my girl!" Mr. Harris cheered. Tyler and Corey fist-pumped each other.

"Wow, so I guess that means *nothing* is impossible. Right, Mr. Harris?" Jenna winked.

Sadie's dad sighed. "Okay, girls. Point taken. You want me to fix the Golden Spoon's roof even if I think it's impossible to fix."

"Who, us?" Kylie replied innocently. "I don't know what you mean…"

Mr. Harris chuckled. "Well, your pal Sadie sure does. She was planning this all along."

Sadie raced to the stands and hugged her family and friends.

"Awesome shot, sis!" her brother Tyler said. "Almost as amazing as my winning basket over the Groton Gators in seventh grade."

"Hey, Dad…" Sadie smiled. "Something to tell me?"

"You won…and you win," her father said. "I'll let Mr. Ludwig know I'll take the job."

Whenever Sadie's cell phone rang at 7 a.m. on a Saturday morning, it was undoubtedly a cupcake emergency.

"Okay, this better be good, Kylie." She yawned and stretched. "I was just in the middle of this awesome dream. I won the WNBA championships, and Michael Jordan was handing me this huge, gold trophy…"

"Rise and shine, Sadie," Kylie chirped. "We have work to do! I just took a huge rush order from Mrs. Lila Vanderwall, president of the New Fairfield Art Society."

"Okay…let me have it. What, when, and how many?" Sadie sighed.

"What you should be asking is how much—as in how much is she willing to pay us to get this order done for a luncheon tomorrow morning. A ton!"

Sadie was suddenly wide awake. "Like how much is a ton?"

"Double our usual price…plus delivery!" Kylie exclaimed.

"OMG! That's awesome! Give me ten minutes to get dressed and grab my apron, and I'll be there!"

When Sadie arrived at Kylie's house, Lexi and Jenna were already in the kitchen.

"This is the plan," Lexi said, handing Sadie a diagram. "We need to do 250 cupcakes celebrating the art society's new exhibit of Moroccan art. Mrs. Vanderwall wants the Moroccan coat of arms on every cupcake. We googled it, and now we need to get rolling on the fondant…"

"We're making ginger spice cupcakes with a ginger mascarpone frosting," Jenna explained. "I'm thinking maybe a pinch of cumin for that authentic Moroccan flavor."

"What should I do?" Sadie said, peeling off her coat and hat, and tying on an apron.

Kylie handed her a carton of eggs. "Get crackin' on that batter!"

The girls needed nearly two hours to perfect the recipe and another two hours to bake and frost the cupcakes. While Jenna and Sadie made sure the cake and frosting had just the right amount of "kick," Kylie and Lexi worked to create a bright yellow, green, and red shield on each cupcake. On either side of the shield were unicorns.

"I think my unicorns need to look more magical," Kylie

suggested, comparing her fondant sculpture to the image they printed off the computer.

Lexi nodded and brushed a unicorn's gold horn with luster dust. "Magical enough for ya?"

After an entire day of baking and decorating, the cupcakes were boxed and ready to be delivered Sunday morning.

"I smell like a Cinnabon." Sadie laughed. "Jenna got more cinnamon on me than in the batter!"

"Well, at least you don't have mascarpone in your hair," Lexi complained.

"Smile and say 'mascarpone cheese,'" Kylie said, snapping a photo on her phone.

The next morning, Mr. Harris drove the girls to the art society and the girls began to unload the cupcakes. There were twenty-two boxes, each one delicately packed with tissue paper between the cupcakes to prevent them from bumping around in Mr. Harris's truck.

"I'm so happy to see that you're prompt," Mrs. Vanderwall greeted them. "I wanted to have plenty of time to set the table perfectly. Please follow me."

She led them through a beautiful room filled with

hand-painted Moroccan tiles in shades of turquoise, orange, and gold. Ceramic pots, plates, and lanterns were arranged in a dazzling array of colors and shapes.

"Wow!" Lexi whispered. "This is amazing!"

"I thought we would display the cupcakes on these authentic Moroccan platters," Mrs. Vanderwall explained, showing the girls to a long rectangular table covered in bright linens.

Lexi opened the first box and gently placed a cupcake in the center of a tray. "Perfect!" she said, examining it.

"What on earth? What *is* that?" Mrs. Vanderwall gasped in horror.

"Um, it's a cupcake?" Kylie replied, confused.

"I ordered 250 cupcakes with the Moroccan coat of arms on them," Mrs. Vanderwall shrieked. "That is *not* it!"

"Oh, no," Kylie winced. "I knew I should have made my unicorns look more magical!"

"There are no unicorns on the Moroccan coat of arms!" the woman screamed. She was fanning herself with an exhibit program and turning a bright shade of red.

Lexi shook her head in disbelief. "We must have made a mistake! They all look so much alike! Do you have a Moroccan coat of arms you can show us?"

Mrs. Vanderwall pointed to a huge flag hanging on the wall. There were two lions on it—and no unicorns.

"What you have made is the Scottish coat of arms," Mrs. Vanderwall sputtered. "I will be humiliated at my luncheon!"

"*Dios mío!*" Jenna whispered. "We are in big trouble!"

"It's not a problem…I promise you, we can fix it!" Kylie tried to calm the flustered woman.

"We can?" Sadie whispered. "We only have two hours until the luncheon!"

"We always carry a repair kit with us in case of a cupcake emergency," Lexi explained. "We'll just take off the horns and reshape and paint the unicorns to look like lions."

"I feel faint…I must sit down!" Mrs. Vanderwall moaned. "My luncheon is ruined…I'm disgraced. Whatever shall I tell the Moroccan prime minister's wife?"

"Don't tell her anything!" Kylie pleaded. "Just give us a chance to fix this!"

While the girls did plastic surgery on the unicorns, Sadie mixed red and yellow food coloring to repaint them a golden hue. The girls all brushed on the color with lightning speed and were just finishing the last cupcake as the first guest entered the room.

"What beautiful Moroccan cupcakes," a lady gushed.

"Oh, I'm so relieved to hear you say that." Mrs. Vanderwall reappeared, mopping her brow with an embroidered hankie. "We're so sorry your husband, the prime minister, couldn't be here to join us as well." She gave the girls a dirty look and escorted her distinguished guest around the exhibit.

Sadie looked down at her shirt, pants, sneakers, and hands. Everything was stained with red food coloring. "I look like a ladybug," she groaned.

"Technically, ladybugs are red with black spots," Jenna corrected her. "Just sayin'…"

"Let's just get our check and get out of here," Sadie sighed.

The girls made their way through the crowd to Mrs. Vanderwall, hoping she'd forgive and forget and hand over their $1,200.

"Well, I'm glad everything worked out and you're happy," Kylie said, putting out her hand to get paid.

"Happy? You nearly gave me a heart attack today! I am anything but happy! And I do not intend to pay you one cent for this frightful experience."

"What? You have to pay us!" Sadie cried. "We worked all day on your cupcakes…"

"And they were wrong. I do not pay for mistakes.

Now leave immediately." She turned her back and stomped away.

"I'm so sorry, Sadie," Kylie said, putting her arm around her friend. "I know you were counting on your share of the money."

Not only was she counting on it, she was planning on using it to buy her new basketball uniform.

"Well, it could have been worse…" Jenna said.

"How?" asked Sadie.

"Give me a minute…I'm working on it."

"I got it: we could have made a coat of arms…with arms on it," Kylie joked. "Like an octopus!"

"I have to *hand* it to you!" Jenna laughed.

"You guys are so corny! Get it? Uni-corny?" Lexi giggled.

Sadie couldn't help but laugh, too. "We got no money… but we're still funny!" she added. No cupcake catastrophe could stop the girls of PLC!

The Heat Is On

Mr. Harris and his crew had worked two weeks on the Golden Spoon—and it was still nowhere near ready to reopen.

"We can't patch the broken rafters. We need to start with brand-new decking," Sadie's dad tried to explain to Mr. Ludwig.

"I don't know what that means…and I don't care," Mr. Ludwig moaned. "Just fix it." The entire store was now covered in ugly black tarp, and Mr. Ludwig couldn't bear to see his beautiful Golden Spoon in such a state of disarray.

"Wow," said Sadie when her dad took her to visit the site. "This is one big hot mess, huh?"

Mr. Harris nodded. "You're not kidding, kiddo. This is some fine job you got me into."

☆ ☮ ☆

"I think my dad is going to kill me for making him repair the Golden Spoon," Sadie told her friends at lunch the next day at school. "It's taking way longer than he thought."

"Tell me about it," sighed Kylie. "Without Mr. Ludwig's order, we're down about $900 in sales these past two weeks."

"That's not good." Jenna whistled through her teeth. "We can't stay in business unless we get more business."

Sadie had done everything she could. Their only option now was to wait for her dad to finish his work on the Golden Spoon—and hope that its customers came back.

The only good news in her life was her math quiz score.

"An A-minus! Sadie, that's wonderful!" her mother declared when Sadie showed it to her after school. "I'm so proud of you."

"I guess I'll have even more time to study with our cupcake business drying up." Sadie sighed.

"I'm so sorry, honey," her mom said as she hugged her. "I know how much it means to you girls. Maybe it'll bounce back."

Sadie went to her bedroom where she could think. She dribbled a ball on the hardwood floor. It was what she did whenever she was worried or upset.

"Money, math, Mr. Ludwig," she repeated with each bounce of the ball. "Mom, Dad, divorce. Peace, Love, Cupcakes."

She threw the ball, and it bounced off the back of her door, just missing the net. She was about to take another shot when her iPod touch rang. It was Kylie calling her on FaceTime.

"Put that ball down, Sadie…we're going to battle!"

"Huh?" Sadie asked. "What are you talking about?"

"Remember that video we sent in auditioning for *Battle of the Bakers*? Well, I got an email today from the producers. They want us to compete in two weeks!"

"Are you serious?" Sadie gasped. "We're going to be on TV?"

They both jumped up and down and screamed.

"I am calling an emergency meeting of PLC tomorrow after school," Kylie said breathlessly. "We need a serious battle plan—and more hands on deck. I'm thinking we should call my camp friend Delaney and get her on board, too. And we'll need to watch every episode from the past three years and take notes."

Sadie's head was spinning, and things got even crazier as soon as Lexi and Jenna heard the news. They came to the teachers' lounge kitchen the next day with a long list of what the club needed for battle.

"Let's start with a dozen more tips for piping," Lexi said. "If we want to look like professionals, we need the right tools."

"And I wrote down key ingredients we have to bring," Jenna said. "Ten types of chocolate, three types of vanilla, some imported spices…"

"Whoa, guys, slow down!" Juliette said. "I think it's fine to create a wish list, but you have to be smart about this. You don't have an unlimited budget."

"But how will we win if we don't have all this?" Lexi insisted. "Those other bakers will be much more prepared."

"You'll do the best with what you have," Juliette replied. "You always have, and your cupcakes are amazing. This isn't a contest about who has more money to spend. It's about being creative and smart."

Kylie sighed. "In other words, we don't stand a chance. We're totally out of our league."

"If the producers thought that, they never would have asked you to compete," Juliette pointed out.

"Maybe they thought we'd provide some comic relief on the show," Jenna said. "We did leave in the part where Sadie got a flour shower."

"They obviously saw star quality in your club," Juliette said. "So let's just be optimistic, and you girls do what you do best: bake cupcakes!"

Kylie thought it would be most efficient to divide and conquer, so she gave each of the girls an assignment. Lexi packed boxes with fondant, modeling chocolate, molds and assorted sprinkles, sanding sugars, and edible glitter. That way, they'd have tons of options for decorating, no matter what the challenge. Jenna was entrusted with all of PLC's recipes. She organized them by theme, flavor, and filling, and printed them out on recipe cards.

Sadie, Kylie, and Delaney divided the sixty-six previously aired episodes of *Battle of the Bakers* between them and took notes on what the judges liked or disliked and what the winners baked. Every episode consisted of two mystery challenges and ingredients—plus a final presentation round for the finalists. The last bakers standing were the winners.

"I'm definitely seeing a pattern," Sadie reported to her clubmates. "The judges hate when you use anything artificial like food coloring. This one baker won with a red velvet cupcake she made with beet juice."

"Eww, gross!" Jenna cried. "No beets are going near *my* cupcakes."

"Then there was this other guy who made a kale cupcake…" Sadie explained.

"Kale?" Delaney made a face. "As in that green stuff?"

"Yup," replied Sadie. "Topped with cream cheese frosting and crushed hazelnuts. The judges said it was 'divine.'"

"Beets, kale…doesn't anyone do a plain, old chocolate cupcake anymore?" Jenna sighed. "Has the entire world gone *loco*?"

"I think it would be fun for you to expand our horizons a little," Juliette suggested. "Beets or no beets, you should get a little creative."

The cupcake club decided a little practice would be a good idea. "Pretend I'm the judge," Juliette instructed. "This is just like *Battle of the Bakers*, girls. I'm going to give you a category, and you'll have sixty minutes to create a cupcake that is both delicious and artistically pleasing."

"I can handle the artistically pleasing part," Lexi said.

"I wouldn't be so sure about that!" Juliette chuckled. "Your category is caveman cupcakes, and your time starts now!"

The girls looked at each other, completely stumped.

"Did cavemen even *eat* cupcakes?" Sadie asked.

"Do you mean real cavemen…or like *The Flintstones*?" Jenna asked.

"Up to you! Any theme could come up on *Battle of the Bakers*," Juliette insisted. "Think outside the box!"

Kylie closed her eyes and tried to picture a prehistoric setting. "I'm thinking swamp beast…" she said.

"Ooh, swamp beast cupcakes. Yum!" Jenna said sarcastically.

"What about mud? Like the Mississippi mud pie cupcakes we once baked?" Sadie suggested.

"Exactly!" said Juliette. "Think about what you've perfected already and how you can adapt it to the theme!"

"We could add marshmallow rocks on top, and I could do different dinos out of chocolate, like a stegosaurus and a T. rex!" Lexi chimed in.

"What about cave paintings? It's a caveman cupcake… let's do some cave paintings on a chocolate cave. We can mold the cave shape by pouring milk chocolate into a funnel!" Jenna added.

"Brilliant, ladies! Get to it!" Juliette called. "You have fifty minutes left!"

They raced around the kitchen, tripping over each

other and spilling batter and chocolate everywhere. When the cupcakes came out of the oven, the cake was rich and gooey, and Jenna piped an extra large mound of chocolate marshmallow frosting on top. In the end, they presented three different cupcakes to Juliette on a platter—each one delicious and elaborately decorated.

"By George, I think you've got it!" Juliette cheered. "You could actually win this, girls!"

"Good thing we didn't make a *Tyrannosaurus wreck*," Jenna joked.

The girls groaned but felt revved and ready for battle!

The Battle Begins!

The night before the *Battle of the Bakers*, Sadie couldn't sleep a wink. She sat on the edge of her bed, dribbling her basketball and trying to go over all the things Juliette told them to remember: stay focused, double-check each measurement before you put in an ingredient, taste everything before you serve it to the judges. It was a lot like cramming for her math test. She knew she had to keep her cool and not panic, even if the clock was ticking down and they had thirty seconds left to finish the round.

When her alarm finally went off at 6 a.m., she grabbed her skateboard, raced downstairs, and waited anxiously at the door for Juliette's car to pick her up and take her to the TV studio. The rest of the audience—including Sadie's parents—would be in the studio for the taping at 10 a.m.

"She's not going to be here for an hour, hon," her mom said, yawning. "You want some breakfast?"

"I can't eat—I'm way too nervous!" Sadie said. "This is huge, Mom. Really huge. This can make or break a cupcake business!"

"I know, Sadie, but I want you to keep things in perspective. It's just a baking contest. It's not the end of the world if you guys don't win. You know that from basketball. It's not whether you win or lose, but how you play the game."

Sadie knew her mom was right, but this felt so much more important than any basketball game she had ever competed in. Maybe it was because PLC was something she had worked so hard to build from the ground up. This was the biggest and best thing that had ever happened to their cupcake club. They just *had* to win!

Juliette pulled up to Sadie's house fifteen minutes early. Kylie was already in the backseat and yanked Sadie in next to her. "Get in! Hurry! We have three more stops to make, and I want to be there super early!"

Sadie was happy to see that her BFF was as much a basket case as she was. "I couldn't sleep," Sadie confided.

"Me neither. I was up counting cupcake wrappers. I wanted to make sure we had enough for all the rounds—just in case we make it to the 500 cupcake finale!"

"Didn't I tell you guys to get some rest?" Juliette sighed. "You're going to fall asleep over your batter."

"Not a chance," Kylie assured her. "I'm not sleeping through PLC's TV debut!"

They picked up Lexi, Jenna, and Delaney and headed on the highway to the show's Westport studios. As soon as they entered the on-ramp, they were in bumper-to-bumper traffic.

"We're never going to get there!" Kylie whined. "Maybe try the right lane…or get off at the next exit and go on local streets?"

"No backseat drivers," Juliette replied. "We'll get there in plenty of time, I promise."

She kept her word: they arrived before any of the other contestants and had time to look around.

"You must be Peace, Love, and Cupcakes." A man wearing a headset rushed over to them. "I'm Jules Goldberg, associate producer."

"What gave us away?" Jenna joked, pointing to their PLC T-shirts.

"Yes, the shirts." Mr. Goldberg nodded. "But I also recognized you from your audition video. Very impressive!"

"We try!" Kylie smiled. "Are we the first bakers here?"

"Oh, yes. I don't expect the others to arrive for a while. This is old hat to them. They pretty much just show up for the taping."

Lexi gulped. "Old hat? You mean all of our competitors have already been on the show?"

"Yes," the producer said, checking his clipboard. "Or on other baking competitions. Or in national championships. We have quite a few champions in the house."

Sadie looked anxiously at Kylie. "Champions? They're putting us up against champions?"

"Relax, girls," Juliette assured them. "You're very well-prepared for *Battle of the Bakers*."

"I'm not so sure about that," Lexi said, picking up a strange plastic tool off a countertop. "I don't even know what this is."

"Um, I believe that is an icing comb," Juliette offered. "You use it for making ridges and swirls on cakes."

"Or for fixing your hair," Delaney said, pretending to touch up her blond ponytail. "Do I look ready for my close-up?"

"Have you ever *seen* a kitchen like this?" Sadie gasped. She glided around the floor on her skateboard. "It's huge! There are like six ovens and four fridges! I'm going to need my skateboard just to get from one end to the other!"

"What do you suppose this does?" Kylie said, picking up a strange tubelike object with a trigger. She pressed a button and a blue flame shot out.

"It's a blowtorch," Juliette said, grabbing it out of her hands. "You use it for desserts like crème brûlée. Do not touch! We don't want to set the place on fire before we even start baking."

Sadie was zipping from corner to corner, checking out the equipment. "And, Sadie, no skateboard," Juliette added. "I'm not sure the judges will appreciate cupcakes on wheels."

"Go on, ladies, get acquainted with your space. Set up your tools," Mr. Goldberg called over his shoulder. "You have plenty of time. I, on the other hand, have camera angles to check."

Three hours flew by as the girls made notes of everything that was in the pantry and tried to figure out how to start the timer on the industrial oven.

"Are you sure it will ring at twenty-two minutes? We don't want our cupcakes to burn!" Kylie said, watching Sadie punch the numbers on the digital panel.

"Kylie, we've practiced a dozen times. It works just fine," Sadie insisted.

"This is just so different from our kitchens at home,"

Kylie added. "It's all so big and modern. I'm used to my mom's old KitchenAid—not this high-tech blender-mixer-thingamajig."

"They really do have everything a baker could want," Juliette said. "It's amazing. You girls should be very excited to have all of this at your fingertips."

"I have never seen so many piping tips." Lexi's eyes were wide. "I think I've died and gone to cupcake heaven."

"That's the spirit," Juliette said. "Think of the possibilities!"

Just then, a noisy group entered the studio.

"OMG!" cried Sadie. "That's him! That's Benny Volero, the Cake King! That guy's won every Food Network competition he's ever been on. He's a pro! He built a replica of the *Titanic* out of cake and sank it in a swimming pool!"

Lexi nodded. "He's a legend. Seriously, how can we ever expect to win against him?"

Sadie glanced across the kitchen set. Benny was signing autographs for the cameramen. He had two commercial mixers, a fondant roller machine, and his own personal piping tips—not to mention a team of six guys in white chef coats. Her stomach did a flip-flop.

"Didn't anyone tell him the kitchen is fully stocked?" Delaney wondered out loud.

"He's Benny. He's the best of the best—so he needs the best stuff," Kylie explained.

"He's not so tough," Jenna piped up. "What's he got that we don't?"

"A hit TV show, a chain of bakeries, about a dozen cookbooks with his name on them…" Sadie sighed. "I think he even has a street named after him in Stamford."

"Oh," Jenna winced. "Good point."

"But what we lack in experience, we make up for in style!" Kylie tried to cheer on her team.

"That's right," Juliette insisted. "You girls have come a long way, and you're going to give these bakers a good fight."

The girls watched as the rest of the bakers filed in. The next ones to arrive were the Connecticut Cupcake sisters, Cece and Chloe.

"They are so organized," Sadie whispered. "Look at all those ingredients in perfect little pink jars and boxes. They even have pink bows in their hair to match!"

Then there was Dina Pinkerton, Sugar Fingers owner and a two-time *Battle of the Bakers* winner.

"Oh, no…not her!" Kylie pretended to bang her head against the kitchen counter.

"The judges love her…we're doomed," said Jenna. "She's a whiz with vegan cupcakes. You can't top her tofu frosting, trust me."

Sadie had to admit the competition looked pretty fierce. How could a group of fifth-graders stand a chance? Then she remembered a basketball game she'd played two years earlier against Rye Country Day School.

"You never know! Sometimes, at the last minute, someone steals the ball," she told her cupcake club.

"There are no basketballs here, Sadie," Kylie reminded her. "Just cupcakes."

"And your skateboard." Jenna giggled.

"My point is I was once up against this *giant* girl from Rye Country Day School," Sadie continued. "She was nine years old and about six feet tall! Everyone thought she was unbeatable. Well, I stole the ball right out from between her hands and I won the game. We creamed those Rye Reptiles!"

"So you're saying there is someone who is actually *taller* than you in elementary school?" Jenna asked. "I don't believe it."

"I think what Sadie is trying to say is 'nothing is impossible,'" Kylie stepped in. "Am I right?"

Sadie smiled. "I knew you'd get it. And I swear, this girl was at least a head taller than me!"

Jerry Wolcott, host of *Battle of the Bakers*, suddenly summoned everyone to attention. "That's my cue to go to my seat in the audience," Juliette said. "Break an egg, girls. Make me proud!"

There was no more time for nerves or self-doubt. "Cupcake bakers, may I please have one representative from each team in the center of the kitchen?" Jerry called. "This person will be the team captain."

Benny strolled over, looking confident. And Cece stepped forward (after she and Chloe thumb-wrestled for it). Kylie looked at Sadie. "You go," she said. "Sadie, you're a real competitor—you know what it takes to win. You never give up."

Sadie gulped. "Me? But Kylie, you're the club president. You should be the leader. Besides, what if they give us something to read? What about my dyslexia?"

Jenna gave her a little push. "Come on, *chica*, you can do it. Put on your game face and get out there!"

Lexi gave her hand a squeeze. "We believe in you, Sadie."

Sadie walked slowly to the middle of the room where three other bakers were gathered, awaiting instructions as the camera crew tested the spotlights. She stood next to Dina Pinkerton, who was adjusting her apron. She looked cool as a cucumber. Sadie nibbled her nails.

"Hey." Dina smiled. "I've heard some great things about your cupcakes."

Sadie smiled back timidly. "Thanks."

"You nervous?" Dina asked.

Sadie thought about what her basketball coach had told her a million times: "Don't let the other team see you sweat. Put on your best game face."

"Um, no, not at all," she lied. "I'm cool." She wasn't sure who she was trying to convince, Dina or herself.

"Good!" Dina replied. "Because I'm a wreck! I am before every competition. But adrenaline is a good thing, you know?"

"It is?"

"Sure! Just try to focus on taste, texture, and presentation, and keep an eye on the clock. And whatever you do, don't put maraschino cherries on your cupcakes."

"Why?" Sadie asked, puzzled.

"Because the head judge, Fiero Boulangerie, *hates* them. You'll lose if you do—trust me!"

Sadie smiled. "Thanks for the tip!"

"I've got another tip for you," whispered Benny. "Make sure your cupcakes have some zip and zing…if you know what I mean."

Sadie scratched her head. "Um, no, I don't know what you mean."

"A little extra excitement—something that takes it over the top," Benny explained.

"Oh!" said Sadie. "Like the time you made a Fourth of July cupcake on *The Cake King* show and it exploded?"

Cece rolled her eyes. "You don't have to throw in all those splashy tricks," she advised. "Just make sure your cupcakes are moist and you use the best quality ingredients. That's how we've become a success."

Sadie tried to take it all in: zip and zing, no cherries, best ingredients. She thought her head was going to explode like Benny's Fourth of July cupcake!

"Places! Places, everyone!" Jerry summoned them. "No more talking. I'd like to introduce you to the judges and then we'll start filming."

Sadie stared out at the audience—it was a packed room. Everyone was watching! Her mom and dad were in the front row, waving at her. Please, Sadie thought, don't let them fight!

Three people walked onto the kitchen set: Fiero, Carly Nielson, owner of Jimmies, the world's first cup-cakery, and…

Sadie gasped. No! It couldn't be!

"I'm sure you know *Battle of the Bakers*' two famous judges, Fiero and Carly," Jerry said. "And our guest judge today is Mrs. Lila Vanderwall, president of the New Fairfield Art Society."

Sadie glanced over her shoulder at her fellow PLC members, who looked as shocked and sick to their stomachs as she felt.

"What's wrong?" Delaney whispered.

"Big *problema*!" Jenna gulped. "Mrs. Vanderwall hates Peace, Love, and Cupcakes! We messed up her order."

"'Messed up' is putting it mildly," Kylie added. "We almost caused an epic art society fail."

"Well, maybe Mrs. Vanderwall has forgotten," Delaney offered. "I'm sure it's all bygones."

Just then, a shriek arose from the judging table: "You! I know you!" Mrs. Vanderwall was pointing an accusing finger at Sadie. "You almost destroyed my event!"

Sadie tried to keep her guard up. "It was an accident," she said softly. "Nice to see you again, Mrs. Vanderwall."

The other bakers looked stunned. They'd never seen a judge get this angry *before* she tasted a single cupcake.

Jerry tried to calm her down by doing a magic trick: he pulled a quarter out of her ear. "Hey, Mrs. V—look at that! *Ears* to you!" Fiero and Carly chuckled.

But Mrs. Vanderwall was not amused. "I do not like magic tricks," she sniffed. "I do not like puns, and I do not like bakers who are unprofessional." She settled into her seat and continued glaring at Sadie.

"Okay…someone needs a little sugar to sweeten her attitude!" Jerry joked. "So let's give it to her. Bakers, here is your first challenge. The first round requires you to make a cupcake that will wow our judges." He pointed to the table piled high with ingredients. "But here's the fun part: you must use two ingredients, one from Section A, one from Section B, that don't go together. This challenge is called The Perfect Pair."

Sadie stared at the table: in Section A, there were tons of snack foods, stuff like potato chips, popcorn, peanut butter, granola, and a mountain of jelly beans. In section B, there were fruits, veggies, hot peppers, and even a jar of pickles.

"Holy cannoli!" Benny cried, mopping his brow. "What are we supposed to do with that?"

"That's for you to bake and us to partake!" Jerry danced around. He pointed to the giant digital clock on the back wall of the studio. "And your time starts *now*!"

Sadie raced back to her team. "What do we want from the table? What can we bake?"

"It's all so yucky," Jenna said. "None of those things go together!"

"Think out of the box, you guys," Kylie pleaded. "There has to be something!"

"What if we do a chocolate potato chip cupcake?" asked Delaney.

"Way too safe," said Lexi. "This is *Battle of the Bakers*. They want creativity. They want to see something that's never been done before. I've watched every episode. Trust me—we need to take a big risk."

"How about popcorn and papaya? Or pickles and Pop-Tarts?" Kylie suggested.

"Eww, eww, and eww!" Jenna insisted. "This has to be yummy or we're heading home in Round 1."

Sadie was the only one not tossing out suggestions. She was too busy looking at the ingredients table, her mind racing a million miles a minute.

"Guys," she said softly. "I think I know what to make."

The girls stopped bickering. "What?" Kylie asked. "Tell us! We only have fifty-five minutes left!"

"My parents are the perfect pair—even though they argue all the time. They belong together."

"We know you're worried about your folks getting divorced," Jenna said. "But what does this have to do with cupcakes?"

"Let's do the two foods my parents like combined in a cupcake. That way we won't just win Round 1, but maybe they'll see what a perfect pair *they* are and won't break up."

The girls were all quiet. "It's a great idea, Sadie," Kylie said, putting her arm around her friend. "But what are their two favorite foods?"

"That's the tricky part," Sadie said. "They really don't go together—but I think we can pull it off." She whispered in Kylie's ear.

"Oh, no. Really?" Kylie sighed. "Okay, let's put it to a quick vote: all in favor of a chili and cheesecake cupcake, raise your hand."

Jenna gasped. "Chili and cheesecake? *Un momento, por favor!* How spicy are we talking?"

"Hot. My dad likes his chili very, very hot. Like three-alarm-blaze hot."

"Ouch!" said Delaney. "We want to wow the judges…not set them on fire."

"I think we can do it," Kylie interrupted. "A sweet, light, cream cheese frosting would balance out the heat of the cupcake."

Jenna nodded. "We could blend some chili spices into a dark chocolate batter. My *abuela* made a delicious 'hot chocolate' cake once. I think I remember how…some cayenne, a little ground chili pepper…"

"And I can make a realistic chili pepper out of fondant and put it on top of the cupcake," Lexi offered.

Sadie cheered. "I knew we could pull it off!"

"Not so fast," Kylie reminded them. "We haven't pulled it off yet. And the clock is down to forty-five minutes."

"Cupcake bakers, opposites attract…but will you repel the judges?" Jerry teased. "Forty-five minutes left!"

"Team PLC," Sadie said, pulling them all into a huddle, just like she'd seen her coach do. "Two-four-six-eight, let's get baking something great!"

Up in the Air

As the cupcake club scrambled to figure out their recipe, the rest of the bakers in the battle were also struggling.

"I said I wanted fresh mozzarella," Benny shouted, throwing shredded cheese at one of his assistants as the cameraman zoomed in for a close-up. "How many times do I have to tell you?"

"Is he making a pizza or a cupcake?" Jenna asked.

"And those sisters do nothing but fight!" Lexi pointed out.

Cece and Chloe were having a tug-of-war in the middle of their kitchen as Mr. Goldberg, the associate producer, instructed the sound technicians to make sure they were catching every word.

"I'm making the frosting," Cece yelled, grabbing a pink bowl out of Chloe's hands. "Mommy says I make the best frosting!"

"Mommy always likes your cupcakes better than mine!" whined Chloe. "But this time I'm doing the frosting!"

"OMG, did you say these people were *professionals*?" Delaney asked. "They sound more like little kids in the school yard!"

"It doesn't matter what everyone else is doing," Kylie said, trying to focus her team. Then she spotted Dina whipping up her signature tofu frosting…and pouring in pickle juice! "Did you guys see that? What is she doing?"

Sadie stepped in and took charge. "Guys, Kylie's right. We have to concentrate on our cupcake!"

"We want this dark chocolate cupcake to have some fire to it," Jenna said. She carefully measured one-eighth of a teaspoon of cayenne pepper and gently mixed it into the batter. "This should do it."

"Are you sure?" Kylie asked. "I mean, are you positive it's not going to set the judges mouths on fire?"

"Remember what Benny told me," Sadie cautioned. "It has to have a little zip and zing…or was it zing and zip? I can't remember!"

"I tasted it three times…it's great," Jenna insisted.

"But does it need to be hotter?" Lexi chimed in. "Sometimes the judges complain they can't taste the heat."

Jenna stepped back from the bowl. "A little faith, please?" she said. "I am the official PLC taster, *sí*?"

"Jenna's right," Kylie said. "We have to get these cupcakes into the oven. We can't second-guess everything."

"Maybe just a pinch more cinnamon?" Sadie pleaded. "My dad's chili is *really* spicy."

Jenna nodded, sprinkled in a pinch more cinnamon, a dash more cayenne, and took a final taste. "*Vámanos!*" she said. "To the oven!"

While they waited for the cupcakes to bake, Lexi and Delaney sculpted tiny fondant chili peppers, and Kylie and Sadie mixed the cinnamon cream-cheese frosting.

"Do we want creamy or whippy?" Kylie pondered, turning on the mixer.

"Definitely whippy," Jenna called. "The lighter and airier, the more it will balance out the richness of the cake."

"Fiero always likes it when frosting melts on his tongue," Sadie recalled. "He said so in at least six episodes."

"Whippy it is!" said Kylie, cranking the mixer to its highest setting.

"Bakers…twenty minutes is all you've got! Will your cupcakes be cool or not so hot?" Jerry called.

"Okay, now that guy is getting on my nerves!" Jenna exclaimed. She stood at the oven door, watching the cupcakes rise. "They have to be the perfect, spongy, moist consistency. Not too dense…not too gooshy."

"What's 'gooshy'?" Delaney asked. "Is that a baking term?"

"It's a Jenna term," Sadie explained. "It means the cake is too lumpy and uncooked in the center."

"I think 'gooshy' sounds better," Jenna insisted. She opened the oven door and stuck a toothpick in the center of a cupcake. When it came out clean, she announced, "*Perfecto!*" and headed for the freezer to cool them down in a flash.

"Ten minutes!" Jerry's voice rang through the studio.

Kylie started to panic. "Oh, no! We need to get them frosted *now!*"

"Keep calm, girls!" Juliette called from the audience.

Lexi had her pastry bag loaded and ready to fire. "Bring 'em out!" she called.

"A few more minutes! They're not cool enough!" Jenna shouted.

"We don't have a few more minutes!" Sadie pleaded. "We need them *now*! Hurry!"

Jenna raced with the baking tray toward the counter. But just as she was about to place the cupcakes down, she stepped on Sadie's skateboard and went sprawling backward. The cupcakes flew out of the tray and into the air.

"Oh, no!" screamed Kylie. "They're going to fall on the floor!"

"I got it! I got it!" Sadie screamed, jumping as high as she could and grabbing two cupcakes in each hand.

"Put them on the plate!" Lexi shouted, as the rest of the cupcakes—and Jenna—landed with a *splat* on the kitchen tiles. Sadie set the cupcakes in front of Lexi, who perfectly swirled the frosting on each of them, sprinkled them with cinnamon, and topped them off with the fondant chili peppers.

"Time's up! Step away from your cupcakes!" Jerry called.

The girls stepped away from the counter, panting and sweating.

"Yow!" yelped Jenna. "Don't step on me! Girl on the floor, remember?"

"That was close...too close!" Sadie tried to catch her breath. She helped Jenna to her feet. "You okay?"

"Lucky for me I had some nice soft cupcakes to break

my fall," Jenna joked. She was covered in dark chocolate cupcake crumbs. "Pretty tasty, if I do say so myself!"

"Ladies and gentleman," Jerry called. "Please present your cupcakes to the judges!"

PLC was up first. "What do I say?" Sadie shook Kylie by the shoulders. "I don't know what to say!"

"Just say what you told us. Explain why this cupcake is The Perfect Pair, just like your parents."

Sadie took a deep breath and approached the judges' table. She knew her parents and her brothers, not to mention everyone at Blakely Elementary, would be home watching them on live TV. Mrs. Vanderwall's lips were tightly pursed, as if she was ready to take a bite out of both Sadie and the cupcake.

"This cupcake is The Perfect Pair because it's inspired by two people who belong together," she said into the camera. "My parents, Bria and Gabriel Harris."

"That's so sweet!" Carly cooed. "Tell us more, Sadie."

"Well, my mom and dad are really opposites. He likes hip-hop music and she likes opera. He watches sports and she loves old romantic movies. Sometimes they fight because they don't see eye to eye, but I know that deep down, they really love each other. This cupcake combines two of their favorite foods that don't really sound like they would go together: spicy chili and cheesecake. But when you combine them in a cupcake…well, they're the perfect pair. Just like my parents."

Sadie held her breath, stared straight ahead, and braced herself for the judges' critiques.

"Zees coopcake…it eez rich…it eez moist…it eez *magnifique*!" Fiero said.

"Did he just say he liked it? I can't understand his French accent!" Delaney whispered.

Carly nodded. "I think the hot chocolaty cake and the light cheese frosting blend together beautifully. I was licking my plate. It was yummy."

Finally, Mrs. Vanderwall raised her fork and took a bite. "Hmmmm…" she mumbled. "Mmmm…..mmmmm…. mmmmm!"

Sadie looked puzzled—was that an "I like it" or an "I hate it"?

"Do you have something to add, Mrs. V?" Jerry asked.

"From an artistic standpoint, the decoration was quite realistic."

Lexi jumped up and down. "Yes! She liked my pepper!"

"But the flavor…it's a *mistake*." She said the last word so loudly that Sadie flinched.

"She will never get over it," Kylie cried. "She's not going to even give us a chance!"

"Why is it a mistake?" Jerry asked.

"I simply don't appreciate spiciness and creaminess together," Mrs. Vanderwall replied. "That's my opinion."

When it was the other contestants' turns, the judges were also divided.

"I think your pickle and parsnip cupcake is clever," Carly told Dina. "But I'm missing some sweetness. I wanted more of a treat."

"Your marinara and marshmallow coopcake…it was a miss for me," Fiero told Benny. "You go too far out of zee box."

Mrs. Vanderwall commended Cece and Chloe for their Pretty in Pink cupcake. "I love the way you created a cloud of cotton candy over the red beet buttercream," she cooed. "Such brilliant use of color."

"Beets," Jenna fumed. "I hate beets!"

But Fiero pointed out that the frosting overpowered their rose-petal-infused cake. "I cannot taste zee flowers," he complained. "Where are zay? Did zay disappear?"

Sadie went back to her team. "I think it's anyone's game," she said. "I'm not sure who will go home first."

"I hope it's not us," said Lexi. "That would be really embarrassing!"

"You did an awesome job presenting, Sadie," Kylie said. "You did your best."

"I hope my parents liked it," she replied. "Do you think they did?"

Kylie shrugged. "They left right after the judging."

"They left?" Sadie gasped. "Why? Are they mad at me?"

"I'm not sure," Kylie said, trying to calm her. "I'm sure it's nothing. Maybe your dad had a work emergency. Or your brother Ty set fire to the toaster again. They just probably had to go and didn't want to distract you."

Sadie hated feeling helpless. She wished she could go back and redo the entire first round—rewind the morning in instant replay mode and change everything. She had probably upset her parents and they were mad or embarrassed. But the judges were already huddled at their table, deciding who would stay and who would go.

"Bakers, please face the judges," Jerry commanded.

"No matter what happens, we're right behind you," Kylie said, patting Sadie on the back.

Jerry held a card in his hands. "I have here the results of Round 1," he began. "One of you is cake royalty...but you failed to make a cupcake that could wow our judges. Benny…I'm sorry. You're done at *Battle of the Bakers*."

Benny's eyes grew wide. "But I'm the Cake King…"

"Yes, yes you are." Jerry shook his hand. "But for now… it's *ciao*!"

"I don't believe it!" Kylie exclaimed. "We made Round 2!"

"It was totally my skateboard wipeout that did it…I'm great on TV," Jenna teased.

"Whatever it was, we really have to bring it in the next round!" said Kylie.

Their cheering section went wild: Kylie's mom and dad waved a big poster that read, "Peace, Love, and Cupcakes is sweet!" and Lexi's big sister, Ava, high-fived Jenna's big sis Gabriella.

"Go, PLC!" Juliette shouted from the audience. Her boyfriend, Mr. Higgins, was also there, giving them a thumbs-up.

"Look! Jeremy came!" Lexi said. "That is sooooo nice!" He and his parents waved from the third row and were seated with Delaney's mom and dad.

Sadie combed the audience for her parents, but there was no sign of them. She didn't have much time to worry, though. Jerry summoned her back to the stage for the next round's instructions. And like Coach always told her, she needed to get her head in the game.

"This round calls for the opposite of your Round 1 creation. For this baking battle, turn your cupcakes upside down. You have ninety minutes! Go!"

Sadie raced back to the kitchen. "I don't get it. Is that some kind of riddle?"

"I don't know," said Kylie. "They've never done this on *Battle of the Bakers* before!"

"Wait, maybe Jenna can fall again and the cupcakes will land upside down on the judges' laps?" Delaney suggested.

"Maybe Jerry means we should reverse what we did with the first cupcake?" Sadie questioned. "Like instead of a hot chocolate cake, make a cold one…"

"And instead of cool frosting, make it hot?" Kylie followed her train of thought.

Jenna shook her head. "No way…it can't be done! In ninety minutes? Not a chance!"

"What? What can't be done?" Delaney asked anxiously.

Sadie shrugged. "It's worth a try. If we pull it off, we'll be the first team to ever do a hot fudge sundae cupcake on *Battle of the Bakers*!"

Cupcakes à la Mode

"Go through that pantry and find us some ice cream!" Sadie said, shoving Delaney toward the freezer.

"We'll need to melt Belgian chocolate on the stove slowly," said Jenna. "It has to pour smooth and thick over the top of the cupcake."

"The ice-cream scoop needs to sit on a cupcake," Kylie added. "What's the best flavor we make?"

"Vanilla bean!" the girls shouted in unison.

"Then vanilla bean it is! Let's get baking!"

Sadie knew the recipe by heart: 2 ¼ cups of flour, 1 ½ cups of sugar, 1 tablespoon baking powder, 1 teaspoon salt, 1 cup of whole milk, 4 eggs, 1 stick of butter, 2 teaspoons pure vanilla extract, and of course, the seeds from one vanilla bean.

"See, you're pretty good with memorizing numbers," Kylie told her. "Ms. Erikka would be proud!"

While the cupcake base baked, Delaney and Jenna worked at the stove, creating the perfect hot fudge sauce. In a pan, they mixed condensed milk, semi-sweet chocolate, and two tablespoons of butter until the mixture took on a smooth, glossy texture.

Once the cupcakes cooled, Sadie placed a scoop of vanilla ice cream on top, and Lexi drizzled the chocolate over it, making a delicate web. "Should we put a cherry on top?" Delaney asked.

"No cherries! No cherries!" Sadie shouted. "Fiero hates cherries." A cameraman shoved a camera in her face, trying to catch her in a moment of panic.

"Yes, thank you, we've got it all under control." Kylie smiled and waved into the lens. Then she whispered to Sadie, "We can't freak out on TV. These cameras are recording everything we do and say."

Instead of cherries, Lexi made a white chocolate peace sign and perched it on top of the fudge and ice cream.

They had only seconds remaining before Jerry called time. "PLC...you presented first last time, so this time you'll be last."

"Oh, no!" Sadie panicked. "The ice cream will melt!"

"Let's hope the other bakers talk really fast," Kylie said,

crossing her fingers. "Or we're going to be serving the judges hot fudge soup!"

Cece and Chloe went first. "Since Carly said our last cupcake needed to be more of a treat, we filled this one with candy!" Cece explained.

Fiero took a bite. "What is zees? I think I cracked my tooth on it!" he cried.

"Oh, that's a gum ball," Cece replied.

"It is like a rock. Zees is bad. Very bad!" he grumbled.

Dina's cupcake was exactly what Jerry asked for: upside down. "I put the frosting in the wrapper, then placed the cake on top," she grinned. "Like a little hat! I call it Topsy Turvy."

"Well, you definitely kept to the theme," Carly said. "But I don't think you gave us anything fresh or new from the last round. I wanted to taste something different. I'm a little over the pickles and parsnips. You didn't work very hard to impress us."

Finally, it was Sadie's turn.

"Well, we decided to make our cupcake the opposite of our first one. The cake is cold—it's ice cream—and the topping is hot—it's fudge."

Fiero looked down at his plate. "And zees? What is zees white thing on top?"

"Oh, that was supposed to be a white chocolate peace sign—for Peace, Love, and Cupcakes," Sadie answered. "I guess it melted."

"My coopcake…it eez soggy. I like the cake part, but the ice cream, it eez how you say…"

"Gooshy!" Jenna shouted from the wings. "I call it gooshy!"

"*Oui*, like the girl says. It eez gooshy!"

Carly put down her fork and used a spoon to taste it. "I have to agree with Fiero. I like the flavor of your vanilla bean cupcake, and the chocolate fudge is divine, but the ice cream made this sad little puddle on my plate."

"Oh, no," Kylie groaned. "She thinks our cupcake is sad!"

As if that wasn't bad enough, Mrs. Vanderwall threw in, "Yes, very disappointing indeed!"

While the judges deliberated, the cupcake club members huddled in their kitchen.

"Don't give up yet," Sadie begged. "Fiero chipped a tooth…maybe they'll be disqualified for that."

Jerry cleared his throat. "Okay, bakers, time to face the judges."

Sadie took her spot in between Cece and Dina.

"This was not an easy decision," Carly began. "We didn't feel that any of the bakers truly baked cupcakes worthy of *Battle of the Bakers* in this round."

Sadie's heart was doing jumping jacks. Had they all failed? Were they *all* going home?

"However, one baker did nothing new to impress us with her cupcake," Carly continued. "Dina…I'm sorry, you're done in *Battle of the Bakers*."

"That's okay…I've won twice. Time to pass the torch!" Dina said. Then she winked at Sadie. "Good luck!"

Rock and Roll

Sadie had no time to let the good news sink in before Jerry started barking orders.

"Cupcake bakers! You have two hours to create a 500-cupcake display. Since you've spent all day learning that opposites attract, we want to see a cupcake display that proves it. You can use a master builder of your own and one additional assistant. Ready...set...bake!"

"We want Mommy to help us!" Cece and Chloe yelled. Their mother appeared from the side of the set, giving them a thumbs-up. "And my husband, Stan, the NASA engineer," Cece said, grinning.

"What do you think Connecticut Cupcake is going to make?" Lexi asked.

"We can't worry about them," Kylie insisted. "Our display has to stand on its own two feet."

"That's it!" Sadie yelled. "Two feet!" She grabbed a

pencil and made a stick figure. Then she drew another on the other side of the page.

"What is that supposed to be?" Lexi said, turning Sadie's drawing upside down. "It looks like a bunny rabbit…or maybe a turtle with a top hat?"

"It's not a bunny or a turtle," Sadie explained. "See? It's a couple?"

"A couple of what?" teased Jenna.

"A man and a woman," Sadie sighed. "You guys…it'll work! Trust me!"

Kylie looked over Sadie's scribbles. "I get it. What if we put them on wheels and push them together? Each one will have his and her own cupcakes, and then in the middle, we'll mix the two together. See…opposites attract."

"And let's make the frosting two different flavors, for example, sweet chocolate and salty peanut butter, so when they come together, they make a beautiful new swirled frosting," said Lexi.

Sadie was relieved that PLC had a game plan, but she was still worried what Cece and Chloe were up to. She looked over and saw their sketch: it was a giant "U" shape covered with mini-cupcakes coated in silver fondant.

"What are they making? A horseshoe?" Delaney asked.

Kylie shook her head. "Not a horseshoe. A giant magnet. It's really clever."

"But our idea is better," Sadie insisted. "If we can build it."

"Did someone say they needed a builder?" came a voice from the edge of the set.

"Daddy?" Sadie gasped. "What are you doing here? I thought you and Mom were mad at me."

"After that sweet presentation? Not a chance!" said Mrs. Harris. "Thank you, Sadie. It was really lovely. We were trying to get backstage to tell you."

Sadie smiled. "So you're not getting divorced?"

"Divorced? Where did you ever get such an idea?" Mr. Harris replied. "Sometimes parents fight when they're stressed, honey. It doesn't mean we're getting divorced."

"We're sorry if we upset you. We're going to try our very best to work things out…together." Mrs. Harris squeezed her husband's hand and smiled. "But for now, you girls have a cupcake battle to win!"

"Dad, can you be our master builder? And Mom, can you be our extra assistant?" Sadie asked. She handed her mother a purple PLC apron.

"We would love to!" her parents said, hugging her.

Sadie stretched out on a big sheet of plywood and lay down on it so Lexi could trace her outline. "You are way too tall!" Lexi laughed. "My hand is getting tired drawing you!"

"The plan is to cut two of these out and then Lexi will paint one to look like a man, the other to look like a woman," Kylie explained to Sadie's father. "Then we'll need to build some shelves so it looks like they're holding the cupcakes in their hands."

"Got it," said Mr. Harris. "And I can put them both on a rolling track so they come together with a light push."

"We still have 500 cupcakes to bake!" Sadie remembered. "And the clock is ticking down!"

"I got the chocolate…" said Jenna.

"I'm on the peanut butter," said Kylie.

"And we'll need a third group that's chocolate with peanut butter filling—I can do that!" said Delaney.

"Wait…Sadie, how many of each type of cupcake do we need?" Kylie asked. "What's the equation?"

Sadie bristled: "How should I know?" *Really?* Did Kylie have to throw math at her now, when they were all under so much pressure?

"Think, Sadie. You can do it. And we need to know how many of each flavor to bake."

Sadie pictured the 500 cupcakes divided into three groups. "Make 166 chocolate and 166 peanut butter. That's almost 14 dozen of each. Then let's do 168 chocolate and peanut butter swirl cupcakes. So 166 + 166 + 168 = 500."

Kylie grinned. "Awesome, Sadie. We're on it!"

By the time the first coat of paint had dried on their display, the cupcakes were coming out of the ovens.

"How are we doing on time?" asked Sadie. She had already piped five dozen chocolate cupcakes with chocolate fudge.

"Less than an hour left," Lexi sighed. "I'm getting nervous. We're so outnumbered!"

"Just keep painting and piping," said Mr. Harris. "I'll get this track working." But as much he pushed and pulled, the two figures refused to roll together.

"I think the weight of the large shelves is slowing them down," he explained. "We need bigger wheels."

Just then, Sadie had a brilliant idea. "Dad, what about my skateboard?"

"That might work," he said, unscrewing the wheels from the board and attaching them to the display. He gave a push and the two figures glided gracefully together in the center.

"Awesome!" Sadie cheered. "Now let's get those cup-cakes on!"

The girls formed an assembly line, passing the cupcakes from Jenna and Lexi down to Delaney, Kylie, and finally Mrs. Harris and Sadie to put on the shelves. "Keep 'em coming. Keep 'em coming!" Sadie coached. "Faster! Faster!"

Jerry was pacing back and forth in front of the giant kitchen clock.

"Three minutes…two minutes…one minute left!" the host called. "Hurry!"

As a buzzer sounded, Sadie placed the last of the 500 cupcakes on the display.

"It's really amazing," Mr. Harris said. "A masterpiece if I ever saw one."

Sadie looked over at the Connecticut Cupcake display. *It* was amazing: a giant spinning magnet covered in metal-lic silver cupcakes. The top of it shot off sparks.

"Wow, that is really cool," Sadie said. "And hard to top. Let's hope the judges agree with you, Dad."

When it was time to reveal the winner, Jerry had all the bakers gather in the center of the studio. "Connecticut

Cupcakes…Peace, Love, and Cupcakes, you both put up a valiant fight. One of you made a giant cupcake magnet that shoots fireworks; the other created a perfect pair that joined together with a chocolate-peanut butter kiss. In the end, only one can take home the prize. Only one can win *Battle of the Bakers*."

Sadie held her breath. Say our name! Say our name! she silently pleaded with him.

"Congratulations…Connecticut Cupcake!" Chloe, Cece, and their mommy jumped up and down, screaming and hugging one another.

Sadie felt like someone had sucked the air out of her… like when she ran over a nail with her bicycle tire. "We lost?" she said. "How could we lose?"

"You girls were amazing," Mr. Harris said. "You're champions in my eyes."

"That's really nice, Dad," said Sadie. "But we didn't win the $5,000. We didn't win the *Battle of the Bakers*."

"It's okay, Sadie." Kylie tried to comfort her. "We were still on TV—which means a lot of people saw PLC and will be ordering our cupcakes."

"Really? Would you want to order cupcakes from a los-ing team?" Jenna moped. "I don't know about you, but I'd be on the phone to Connecticut Cupcake ordering a dozen of those Pretty in Pinks."

Juliette ran up from the audience and gave them each a hug. "Good job, girls. You really looked and acted like pros out there. I am so, so proud of you all!"

When Sadie got home, every muscle ached. She flopped down on her bed, not having the energy to even take off her frosting-stained apron and clothes.

"You look like you've been through a war," her brother Tyler remarked.

"Not a war. A battle. I can't move."

"I saw you on TV. The cupcake you did for Mom and Dad? That was pretty cool." It wasn't very often that her brother paid her a compliment.

Sadie smiled. "Thanks. I really want things to get better for our family."

"They will," Tyler said, patting her on the shoulder. "Money may be tight, but the Harrises put up a fight!"

"I'm glad you're getting A's in math," Sadie teased. "Because you are one awful poet!"

"Seriously, little sis, you know it's gonna be okay, right?"

Tyler gave her arm a playful punch. "Dad says we're just going through a rough patch. And you know he's really good at smoothing out rough patches with sandpaper."

Just then, Sadie remembered: the Golden Spoon roof!

"I almost forgot!" she said, jumping off her bed. She suddenly felt a second wind of energy—maybe her father had some good news. "Thanks for the pep talk!" She gave her brother a punch back.

"*Ow!* Take it easy! That hurt!" Tyler whined.

"Wimp!" Sadie giggled, and headed downstairs.

She found her father hunched over his desk, looking over blueprints.

"Hey, Dad…I could sure use some good news. How's the Golden Spoon coming?"

"Oh, it's coming…slowly and surely," he answered. "Mr. Ludwig likes to change his mind a lot, so I had to make some revisions. But I think you and your friends should put a week from Sunday on your calendar."

"What's that?" Sadie asked.

"The grand reopening of the Golden Spoon in Greenwich!"

The Icing on the Cake

Jenna thumbed through PLC's recipe file, searching for the perfect cupcake to bake for the Golden Spoon's grand reopening party.

"It should be something golden delicious," she said.

"Like the apple?" asked Delaney.

"No...like a golden cake. How 'bout this?" Jenna pushed a recipe card in front of Kylie.

"A lemonade cupcake? Well, it's definitely the right color..."

"How about pineapple? Or banana?" Delaney suggested.

Lexi shook her head. "We've done those tons of times. It's such a special occasion that we should do something really spectacular."

Sadie took a stack of recipe cards from Jenna and flipped through them. "No, no, no....*yes!*"

She pulled a card out and placed it on the table in front of her friends.

"Whoa…that looks awesome," Jenna said. "But we've never tried it like that before."

"How hard could it be?" Kylie pondered, skimming the ingredients. "It's a basic golden cake and caramel oozes out of the center…makes my mouth water just thinking about it!"

"I love the gold sugar crystals on the frosting," Lexi said. "Too bad we don't have one of those fondant printers like the Cake King had. We could do the Golden Spoon logo on top."

"All agreed…say 'cupcake'!" Kylie said.

"CUPCAKE!" everyone yelled, seconding the motion.

Six hours later, Sadie, Mrs. Harris, and the girls were helping her father load his truck with twelve dozen Golden Caramel cupcakes.

"You're gonna save me one, right?" Mr. Harris asked his daughter.

"Are you kidding? After all the hard work you did on the Golden Spoon? You can have two!" Sadie hugged him.

When they arrived in Greenwich, a big crowd was already lined up outside the door.

"Wow," Kylie remarked. "Looks like Mr. Ludwig's customers missed him!"

"Or they missed PLC's cupcakes," Mrs. Harris pointed out.

They piled out of the truck and knocked on the door. Mr. Ludwig was watching out the window with a huge smile on his face. "You're here! You're here! Please come in!"

Sadie had never seen him so excited. He practically skipped to the door to open it. He was dressed in a lavender suit with a metallic gold tie.

"Close your eyes," he insisted. "Don't look just yet!"

The girls obeyed as Mr. Ludwig guided them through the door and into the store.

"You, too!" Mr. Harris said, covering his wife's eyes. "No peeking!"

"I feel like I'm on an episode of *Extreme Makeover: Home Edition*," Mrs. Harris said, chuckling. "What do you have up your sleeve, Gabe?"

The store smelled like wood chips and fresh paint, one of Sadie's favorite aromas.

"Okay…open them!" Mr. Ludwig commanded.

The girls couldn't believe their eyes! The entire store had been painted a beautiful shade of purple. There were brand-new glass shelves from floor to ceiling, a crystal chandelier dangling from the ceiling, and in the very front, a giant display for Peace, Love, and Cupcakes.

"OMG!" Kylie gasped. "We get our own cupcake display?"

"Well, I thought having cupcakes at the Golden Spoon every week from the finalists for *Battle of the Bakers* would be a big draw for my customers." Mr. Ludwig winked.

"Dad, you did an amazing job!" Sadie exclaimed. The display looked like a giant cupcake with glass shelves from top to bottom.

"And you'll notice I did a peace sign on top...not a cherry," Mr. Harris added. "I know how Fiero feels about maraschino cherries."

Just then, Fiero, Carly, Jerry, *and* Mrs. Vanderwall stepped forward.

"You're here? You came?" Sadie said breathlessly. Dina, Cece, and Chloe were also there to celebrate.

"Well, zees gentleman said he has zee finest coop-cakes—so we had to taste for ourselves," Fiero said.

"And now that we see who makes them, I'm sure we won't be disappointed." Jerry smiled. "Right, Mrs. V?"

Sadie opened the box and handed her a Golden Caramel cupcake.

Mrs. Vanderwall took a lick…then another…then another.

"Mmmmm," she said. "Mmmmm….mmmmmmm."

Kylie elbowed Sadie. "That's a definite 'I like it'!"

"You know, I discovered these girls," Mr. Ludwig began. "They owe it all to me."

"Here we go!" Jenna groaned.

"I have an incredible talent for finding culinary talent…"

"*Oui?* You like zee French macaroons?" Fiero interrupted.

"Do I like them? I love them!" Mr. Ludwig cried. "I could talk food for hours!"

"Then we'll be here a very, very long time," Mr. Harris whispered and tugged on Sadie's ponytail. "I can't understand a word that Fiero guy says!" He took Sadie's chin in his hand. "Did I mention how proud I am of you?"

"Yeah…a couple dozen times," Sadie said, blushing.

"We're proud of all of you," Jerry jumped in. "Which is why *Battle of the Bakers* decided to award you this." He handed Sadie a large white envelope.

"What is it?" she asked.

"Open it! Open it!" the girls screamed.

Inside was a check for $500—and a certificate that read, "In Special Recognition of *Battle of the Bakers'* Youngest Finalists: Peace, Love, and Cupcakes."

"OMG!" Kylie squealed. "So we're winners?"

"Apparently so," sniffed Mrs. Vanderwall. "I suppose even Michelangelo made a few mistakes now and then."

"That will cover the cost of the fondant printer we wanted," Lexi said. "Just think of all the awesome stuff we can make now!"

"With a display this size, I expect you to fill it weekly," Mr. Ludwig reminded them.

Sadie was thrilled—but not just over the check and the certificate and the crowd of customers gobbling up their cupcakes. She noticed that her mom and dad were not only getting along, they were holding hands in the corner of the Golden Spoon. Her mom was oohing and ahhing over her dad's handiwork, and they looked happy for the first time in a long time.

Kylie tossed her a cupcake, and Sadie caught it in one hand. She took a bite and savored the moment.

"Pretty good, huh?" Kylie asked her.

"Not just good…" Sadie smiled, licking the sticky caramel off her fingers. "Golden!"

Turn the page for three delicious PLC recipes, plus a sneak peek at the club's next adventure!

"No Business Like Snow Business"
Snowball Coconut Cupcakes

Snowball Coconut Cupcakes
Makes 14

- ½ cup sweetened coconut flakes
    - + 2 tablespoons for garnish
- ½ cup butter, at room temperature
- ¾ cup sugar
- 1 ½ teaspoons vanilla extract
- 2 eggs
- 1 ½ cups all-purpose flour
- 1 ½ teaspoons baking powder
- ¼ teaspoon salt
- ½ cup coconut milk
- ½ cup sour cream

Directions

1. Preheat oven to 350°F. Place 14 cupcake liners in a cupcake pan.

2. Toast the coconut flakes on a cookie sheet for 10 minutes, or until golden brown.

3. In an electric mixer, cream butter and sugar until light and fluffy. Add in the vanilla extract and eggs, beating after each addition.

4. In a separate bowl, sift together the flour, baking powder, and salt. Add the dry mixture to the butter mixture, alternating with the coconut milk.

5. Beat in sour cream and toasted coconut flakes.

6. Fill cupcakes ¾ of the way. Bake for 16-18 minutes, or until a toothpick comes out clean.

7. Let cupcakes cool.

8. Once cupcakes are cooled, cut a circle about ½ inch deep out of the middle of the top of each cupcake.

9. Spoon Vanilla Meringue Frosting into the cut cupcakes.

10. Frost with Vanilla Meringue Frosting, and sprinkle with toasted coconut.

Vanilla Meringue Frosting

Makes 3 cups frosting

   4 large egg whites

   A pinch of salt

   1 cup of confectioners' sugar

   2 teaspoons vanilla

   ¼ teaspoon cream of tartar

Directions

1. Fill a pot half full with water. Simmer water.

2. Place a bowl on top of the pot, large enough so that it does not fall in or touch the water. Whisk all ingredients together in the bowl until the mixture is hot, about 2 minutes.

3. Take the mixture off the water and pour into an electric mixing bowl. Using the electric mixer, beat the hot egg mixture on high speed for 5 minutes, or until the mixture has cooled and stiff peaks have formed.

Golden Caramel Cupcakes with Caramel Buttercream Frosting

Golden Caramel Cupcakes

Makes 16

    ¾ cup unsalted butter, softened

    1 cup sugar

    3 eggs, separated

    ½ teaspoon vanilla extract

    1 cup all-purpose flour

    ½ teaspoon baking powder

    ½ teaspoon baking soda

    ½ teaspoon salt

    ¾ cup buttermilk

    1 cup Caramel Drizzle (recipe follows)

    2 teaspoons gold sugar crystals

Directions

1. Preheat oven to 350°F. Line muffin tins with cupcake liners.

2. In a large bowl, cream butter and sugar until light and fluffy. Add egg yolks, one at a time, mixing until incorporated.

3. Add the vanilla, and mix until all ingredients are combined.

4. In a smaller bowl, sift together the flour, baking powder, baking soda, and salt. Add the dry mixture to the butter mixture, alternating with the buttermilk; end with the flour.

5. In a separate bowl, beat the egg whites until stiff peaks form. Fold into cake batter.

6. Pour 1 teaspoon of Caramel Drizzle into each liner. Add cupcake batter on top.

7. Fill cupcakes ¾ full. Bake 20 minutes, or until a toothpick comes out clean. Let cool in pan.

8. Allow cupcakes to cool. Once cool, fill a pastry bag or a squeeze bottle with half of the caramel. Push the tip into the cupcake and squeeze the caramel drizzle into the center.

9. Frost with Caramel Buttercream Frosting. Use a spoon to lightly drizzle on Caramel Drizzle, and sprinkle with gold sugar crystals.

Caramel Buttercream Frosting

Makes 3 cups frosting

   2 sticks unsalted butter, at room temperature

   4 cups confectioners' sugar

   A pinch of salt

   1 tablespoon vanilla extract

   1 tablespoon milk

   3 tablespoons Caramel Drizzle

Directions

1. Beat the butter until smooth.

2. Add confectioners' sugar and salt. Beat until most of the sugar is moistened, scraping down the sides of the bowl once or twice.

3. When the mixture is fully combined, add vanilla, milk, and Caramel Drizzle.

4. Increase speed and beat until light and fluffy, about 4 minutes.

Caramel Drizzle

Note: If making Caramel Drizzle, please have adult supervision and use caution when melting sugar. You can also substitute with a jar of store-bought caramel sauce.

Makes 1 cup Caramel Drizzle

    1 cup sugar
    6 tablespoons butter
    ½ cup heavy cream

Directions

1. Heat sugar on medium-high heat in a medium-sized sauce pan. As the sugar begins to melt, constantly stir with a wooden spoon.

2. Stop stirring as soon as the sugar begins to boil. Once all of the sugar is melted, add the butter and whisk until all the butter is melted.

3. After the butter has melted, take the mixture off the heat. Count to five and very slowly add the heavy cream to the pot, stirring constantly. At this time, the mixture will dramatically increase.

4. At this point, the caramel will be extremely hot. Let cool until room temperature and refrigerate to thicken.

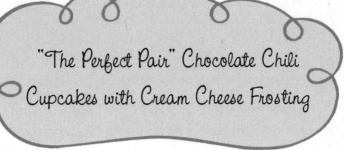

"The Perfect Pair" Chocolate Chili Cupcakes with Cream Cheese Frosting

Chocolate Chili Cupcakes

Makes 12

- 1 cup all-purpose flour
- ½ cup cocoa powder
- 1 cup sugar
- 1 teaspoon baking soda
- 1 teaspoon baking powder
- ½ teaspoon salt
- ¼ teaspoon cayenne pepper
- 1 egg
- ½ cup milk
- ¼ cup vegetable oil
- ½ teaspoon vanilla
- ½ cup warm water
- 2 tablespoons cocoa powder, for dusting

Directions

1. Preheat oven to 350°F. Line the muffin pan.

2. Mix together flour, cocoa powder, sugar, baking soda, baking powder, salt, and cayenne pepper.

3. Add the eggs, milk, oil, vanilla, and warm water. Mix until smooth and combined.

4. Divide batter evenly among the cups, filling each ¾ full.

5. Bake until a toothpick comes out clean, about 15 minutes.

6. Cool cupcakes and frost with Cream Cheese Frosting.

7. Lightly sift cocoa powder on top.

Cream Cheese Frosting

Makes 2 cups frosting

    4 tablespoons unsalted butter at room temperature

    1 cup cream cheese

    4 cups of confectioners' sugar

    2 teaspoons vanilla

Directions

1. Beat the butter and cream cheese until smooth.

2. Add confectioners' sugar and salt. Beat until most of the sugar is moistened, scraping down the sides of the bowl once or twice.

3. When the mixture is fully combined, add vanilla.

4. Increase speed and beat until light and fluffy, about 4 minutes.

Recipes developed by Jessi Walter, Founder and Chief Bud at Taste Buds Kitchen (www.tastebudskitchen.com).

Carrie's Tips for Throwing Your Own Cupcake Challenge!

It's a lot of fun to stage a baking battle in your own kitchen. I've done it tons of times with friends—and the best part is eating whatever you make! Everyone's a winner!

1.   Divide your friends into two or three teams—and pick a name for your teams. For example, "Sweet Sensations" or "Cupcake Queens." I like to make a poster with our team name on it. It puts you in the mood!

2.   Pick older members of your family—like your mom, dad, or siblings—to be the judges. (Younger ones can help, too.) The adults can also help you put cupcakes in the oven and take them out.

3.   Come up with a theme for the cupcake battle. I've done lots of different themes, like "Pirates and Princesses," "Easter Eggs," and "Haunted Halloween." I've even done one to celebrate the royal wedding in England!

Any occasion or idea is a great one! I decide ahead of time so I can provide my friends with cupcake decorations and wrappers that match the theme.

4. Set the timer for *exactly* 60 minutes. The cupcakes should take about 20 minutes to bake, which leaves you enough time to mix, cool, decorate, and display your cupcakes. Pick one flavor to bake for both teams (unless you have two mixers and can make two flavors).

5. Your team gets to decide how they will color, fill, and frost the cupcakes. Here's how you set yourself apart from the competition! For Halloween, we made gross green frosting ooze out of a chocolate cupcake. Then we put gummy spiders on top. Make sure each team has a lot of choices: fill small cups with different types of candies, sprinkles, and chips. You can also provide food coloring (to dye your cupcake batter) and fondant (to make small figures or decorations).

6. Make sure the judge sets a timer and tells you every 5 to 10 minutes how much time is remaining. It's a lot of fun when you know the clock is ticking down…that makes it even more exciting and like a real cupcake battle.

7. After you have frosted your cupcakes, display them creatively. I have a cupcake tower so I love to stack

mine high. You could also serve them in a circle, on a silver platter, with bows around the wrapper, any way you think will impress the judges!

8. Finally, ask your judges to rate the cupcakes on taste, decoration, and theme. I like to give the winner a cupcake-themed prize, like some pretty cupcake wrappers or a cupcake charm. Congrats!

For more cupcake news, reviews, recipes, and tips, check out Carrie's website: www.carriescupcakecritique .shutterfly.com and Facebook page: www.facebook.com/ PLCCupcakeClub. You can also email her at carrieplcclub@ aol.com.

Here's a sneak peek of the
next book in the Cupcake Club,

Icing on the Cake

Girls start your ovens!
The Cupcake Club is back with an even sweeter
story and mouthwatering recipes to match!

The girls of Peace, Love, and Cupcakes volunteer to make a giant cupcake wedding tower for Jenna's mom's wedding in Las Vegas. But in the midst of all the excitement, Jenna has mixed emotions about her new family. She's worried that her new stepdad will want to move the family closer to his work and she doesn't want to leave her school or her friends. Meanwhile, the girls' new teacher, Juliette, announces she's getting married, too. And she wants PLC to make the cupcakes for the reception! Will the girls be able to pull off two weddings in just one weekend?

The aroma of her madre's *magdalenas* rising in the oven made Jenna Medina open her eyes and leap out of bed—even though it was 6 a.m. on a Sunday and the sun was barely up. The light, sweet muffins with just a hint of lemon zest were one of her favorite breakfasts and her mom's specialty, usually reserved for special occasions. It wasn't her birthday…or any of her siblings'. So why the special treat?

"Where are you going?" her big sister Gabriella grumbled. "It's too early."

"Go back to sleep," Jenna whispered. She hoped her Mami would give her a delicate pastry right out of the oven before they were all gobbled up. That was the thing about having two older sisters and twin younger brothers—you had to fight for your share of practically everything, from food to clothes to the TV remote.

"As if I could ever sleep with all the snoring that goes on in this room!" Gabby gestured to the bunk bed above her, where her oldest sister, Marisol, was making a loud, hissing sound through her nose.

"She's worse than you are…and that's saying a lot!" Gabby groaned. She pulled the pillow over her head, trying to drown out the racket. Sharing a room with two sisters wasn't easy!

"*Buena suerte*…good luck!" Jenna chuckled. She

wrapped the purple fuzzy cupcake robe her BFF Kylie gave her for Christmas over her PJs. "I'm going to see what Mami is up to."

She tiptoed down the hall of their small apartment. She could hear her mother banging around in the cupboard. Uh, oh, Jenna suddenly thought. I hope we didn't use up all her sugar on our last cupcake order.

Peace, Love, and Cupcakes—the club and cupcake business Jenna and her four friends Kylie, Lexi, Sadie, and Delaney ran while trying to be normal fifth graders— had a knack for baking up a storm. Their last batch of St. Patrick's Day cupcakes had used up four dozen of her mom's eggs, Jenna recalled. Not to mention all that food coloring, flour, and vanilla extract. Kylie was sure she had bought enough to make their weekly order of 200 cupcakes for The Golden Spoon gourmet shop and four more dozen custom orders. But then Lexi decided she needed to experiment more with the color of the icing.

"I'm not sure I like the green," she sighed, piping it on a vanilla cupcake. "Does it say St. Patty's or split pea soup to you?"

Jenna shrugged. "It kinda says 'spinach stuck in your teeth' to me. I'd put in a little more blue—but you're the artist."

Lexi closed one eye and squinted out of the other. "I say....back to the drawing board!" Jenna wasn't surprised; when it came to icing color, Lexi was very picky.

Each of the girls in the club had a special talent: Lexi created beautiful fondant decorations and elegant swirls of frosting on each cupcake. Sadie was the most coordinated, able to crack and egg in one hand while stirring chocolate on the stove with the other. Kylie was the club's president—which meant she kept track of orders, organized meetings and baking schedules, and generally kept everything running smoothly (most of the time!). Jenna liked to think of Kylie as PLC's "lemon zest"—she added a "kick" to the club, whenever they needed a little push or inspiration. She reminded them what was really important ("friends and frosting!").

Delaney—who joined PLC after Kylie met her in sleep-away camp—had become the club's DJ. Anytime the girls were stressing over a crazy deadline, she'd crank up her MP3 player and break into song and dance (usually Lady Gaga, Katy Perry, or Adele). It was so much fun, and got everyone pumped up. When Jenna complained last week that she was tired of the usual soundtrack and wanted some Latin rhythms, Delaney obliged. She jumped on the couch and sang J.Lo's "Let's Get Loud" into a wooden spoon. Delaney was a riot—and the only person she knew who could sing the entire "Gangnam Style" in the original Korean!

"How did you memorize that?" Sadie gasped. "I can barely memorize my multiplication tables!"

Delaney smiled. "I am a whiz with lyrics. Anything I need to learn, I sing. I got a 98 on my American History test because I could rap the entire Preamble!"

Then there was Jenna. Kylie made her the official "taster" for the cupcake club right after their first meeting. Jenna had to admit she had some talented tastebuds. She could tell with one bite what type of vanilla (Madagascar? Tahitian? Mexican?) or brand of chocolate (Callebaut from Belgium? Amadei from Italy? El Rey from Venezuela?) went into a cake batter. While other kids at Blakely Elementary teased her about being overweight, her friends never judged her. That was the thing about PLC: everyone appreciated each other for the unique talents they possessed—and the special people they were.

And in a family of five kids where she landed smack in the middle, being appreciated was all Jenna ever wanted. She felt most of the time like she got lost in the crowd. She wasn't as pretty as Gabby or as smart as Marisol. And her twin brothers, Enrique and Emanuel, were just too much trouble to compete with. They were seven years old and in first grade at Blakely. Kylie nicknamed them "Tweedle Dee and Tweedle Dum," but Jenna preferred "The Disaster Duo." Wherever they went, chaos followed.

This morning was no different: the living room looked like a tornado had swept through it. There were toys, blocks, sneakers—even a tube of toothpaste—scattered around the room. Manny was busy building with Legos in a corner and Ricky....where was Ricky?

"You the only one up?" Jenna asked, peering behind the sofa and in the closet. Ricky loved to jump out and scare her to death, and she suspected that's what he was plotting.

"He's with Mami mixing cake," Manny pointed to the kitchen. "He says he's going to join your cupcake club."

Jenna bristled at the thought. That's all she needed: her crazy little brother finger painting the walls of Blakely with frosting. She knew Kylie would feel the same, but Juliette, their club advisor, always reminded them "the more the merrier." She didn't think anyone who wanted to join a club should be excluded. She had never met Ricky.

"Cake? You mean *magdelenas*. My favorite Spanish sweet!" Jenna replied.

"No. She said it's a wedding cake."

Jenna looked puzzled. "A wedding cake? Why would Mami be making a wedding cake?"

Manny scratched his nose—that's what he did whenever he was thinking something over. "Dunno."

"Ay, *dios mio*!" Jenna exclaimed. It was her Spanish version of "OMG." She would have to get to the bottom of this.

She barged through the kitchen door and found her mother and Ricky at the counter frosting a white cake.

"*Buenos dias, mija*!" her mom smiled brightly.

Ricky held up his hands, covered in frosting. "*Hola*, Jenna!"

"Everyone is up so early today," said a voice behind her. It was her mother's boyfriend, Leo. Jenna spun around and gave him an icy stare. What was *he* doing here?

He tried to kiss her on the top of her head, but Jenna pulled away. Hadn't she made it clear every time he was here that she didn't like him? She'd practically ignored him the entire Christmas Eve dinner, keeping her face buried in her plate of *cordero asado*—her mom's famous roast lamb.

"You're very quiet, Jenna," Leo remarked. "Hope you're

not feeling baaaa-d." Manny and Ricky cracked up and began making more barnyard animal sounds.

Jenna didn't glance up once from her plate. She didn't know what her mother saw in this guy! He thought he was funny...but he wasn't. And no one was about to out-pun her.

She picked up a plate of veggies and pushed it under his nose. "Would you like some? You know what they say at the holidays: 'Peas on Earth, good will towards man?'"

Leo slapped his hand on his thigh. "Now *that's* a great one!" he laughed out loud. "But I find your mother's orange flan more a-pealing. Get it? Oranges are a-pealing?" He continued to laugh till his cheeks turned red and his eyes watered.

Jenna glanced around the table: everyone was cracking up at his dumb joke. Everyone except her.

"He's very handsome and smart," Marisol leaned over and whispered. What did she know? She was a freshman in high school and totally boy crazy!

"And he works in manufacturing for Ralph Lauren, the famous fashion designer," Gabby sighed. "Do you think he could get me that red gown Taylor Swift wore to the Grammy's for my middle school dance?"

Jenna's mom was just as smitten as her sisters. From the moment Leo came into her cleaning store and remarked how beautiful and neat her stitches were, she was practically head over heels.

"We have so much in common," she told Jenna. "We both love fashion, and the Yankees, and food! Leo loves my cooking!"

Well, that was clear! He made himself a guest in their apartment every other Friday night for dinner—whenever it was his ex-wife's turn to take their daughter.

"He's such a devoted Papi to his little girl," her mom cooed.

Jenna's dad was anything but devoted. The way she remembered it, he had packed his bags suddenly one day when she was five years old and the twins were babies. He was always traveling for work, so goodbyes were nothing unusual. She remembered that he simply kissed her on both cheeks and walked out the door. No explanation; no long goodbye. Most of the other details were fuzzy: her mom crying, her sister Marisol standing at the door and waiting for him to return. But he never did. It was like he simply vanished off the face of the Earth. She knew Marisol pretended he was dead—at least that's what she told her friends. But Jenna knew the truth—her *abuela* had shared it when she came to visit her relatives in Ecuador last summer.

"Do you want to talk to him?" her grandmother asked her one day. "He lives in Ecuador. He has another family now. But I can call if you like."

Jenna shook her head. "No. He's gone." She could never forgive him and she didn't need him. The Medinas stood by each other and they survived. Jenna's mom got a job as a seamstress in a dry cleaning store, and her two sisters worked there after school and on weekends when they got older. They didn't have a lot of money or a lot of "stuff," but they had each other, and that's all they ever needed.

Until *he* came along.

"Leo's a really nice guy," Marisol told her. "He makes Mami happy."

Jenna wanted to see her mother happy. She wanted to see her not working so hard all the time and falling asleep in her armchair in the living room before the evening news. But she wasn't convinced that Leo was the answer. He tried too hard—and it got on her nerves.

On her birthday in January, he showed up with an extravagant present. "I hear you're a Yankees fan like your mother," he said. He tossed her an autographed ball. "That's A. Rod's signature."

Jenna caught it and rolled it between her fingers. "Wonder how much I can get for this on Ebay?"

"Jenna!" her mother scolded her in Spanish. "*Dar las gracias*!"

But Jenna wasn't about to say "Thank you" or apologize for how she felt. Nothing he could do or say would ever change that. But Leo kept pushing.

Today, he was determined to show his expertise in the kitchen. This should be good for a laugh, Jenna smirked. He tied on one of her mother's aprons and stuck a finger in the vanilla frosting.

"Hmmm, *delicioso*!" he said, taking a lick. He then kissed her mother on the lips. Jenna wrinkled her nose and turned away.

"I see where you get your baking talent from, Jenna," he added. "You know my daughter Madison is your age. I told her about your cupcake club and she said it sounded—I quote—'awesome.' Maybe she could join your club?

First Ricky wanted to join PLC…now 'Maddie'? Things were getting worse by the moment!

"You like my cake?" her mother asked Leo.

"It's *bonita*, Betty…just like you."

If they kiss again I'm going to scream! Jenna thought.

"It's a wedding cake," Ricky piped up.

"No, not a wedding cake. An engagement cake," her mother corrected him.

"Why are you baking an engagement cake? Who's engaged?" Jenna asked. Something told her she didn't want to hear the answer.

Her mother smiled and held out her hand. On it was a sparkly pear-shaped diamond ring. "I am!"

Acknowledgments

Hugs and sprinkles go out to:

Our loving family: the Kahns, Berks, and Saperstones. (Jason, when are you making the movie version?)

Our *amazing* recipe developer, Jessi Walter of Taste Buds. (Now a Mrs.! Congrats!)

Our PS 6 family, especially Ms. Fontana, Ms. Levenherz, and Ms. Errico.

Carrie's BFFs: Jaimie Ludwig and Darby Dutter—what would I do without you two?

The BAE Level 3 girls, especially Julia Applebaum and Alexa Malone (stretch, girls!); and PS 6 pals Delaney Hannon, Abby Johnson, Ava Nobandegani, Brynn and Dale Heller.

Carrie's Camp Hillard crew: Julia Goldberg, Reina McNutt, Rebecca Pomerantz, Jessica Roth, Sara Binday, Allison Lax, and Erin Donahue. *Grease* is the word! And Gabby Borenstein—my fave Hillard counselor forever!

Sheryl's supporting cast: Holly Russell, Kathy Passero, Stacy Polsky, Pam Kaplan, Michele Alfano, and Debbie Skolnik.

The cupcake experts who have been so supportive of *Carrie's Cupcake Critique*: Katherine Kallinis and Sophie LaMontagne of *DC Cupcakes*; *Cake Boss* Buddy Valastro; Doron Petersan of Sticky Fingers, and Rachel Kramer Bussel and Nichelle Stephens of the *Cupcakes Take the Cake* blogspot.

The folks at Sourcebooks Jabberwocky—we couldn't ask for a better team to work with! Steve Geck, Derry Wilkens, Leah Hultenschmidt, Aubrey Poole, Helen Nam, and Jillian Bergsma.

Illustrator extraordinaire Julia Denos for bringing the PLC characters to life on every cover.

Our agents at the Literary Group: Frank Weimann, Katherine Latshaw, and Elyse Tanzillo.

About the Authors

Photo by Heidi Green

New York Times bestselling co-author of *Soul Surfer*, Sheryl Berk was the founding editor-in-chief of *Life & Style Weekly* as well as a contributor to *InStyle, Martha Stewart,* and other publications. She has written dozens of books with celebrities including Britney Spears, Jenna Ushkowitz, and Zendaya. Her 10-year-old daughter, Carrie Berk, a cupcake connoisseur and blogger, cooked up the idea for The Cupcake Club series while in second grade. Together, they have invented dozens of crazy cupcakes recipes in their NYC kitchen (can you say "Purple Velvet"?) and have the frosting stains on the ceiling to prove it. They love writing together and have many more adventures in store for the PLC girls!

Peace and Love and CUPCAKES

Meet Kylie Carson.

She's a fourth grader with a big problem. How will she make friends at her new school? Should she tell her classmates she loves monster movies? Forget it. Play the part of a turnip in the school play? Disaster! Then Kylie comes up with a delicious idea: What if she starts a cupcake club?

Soon Kylie's club is spinning out tasty treats with the help of her fellow bakers and new friends. But when Meredith tries to sabotage the girls' big cupcake party, will it be the end of the cupcake club?

Book 1

Recipe For Trouble

Meet Lexi Poole.

To Lexi, a new school year means back to baking with her BFFs in the cupcake club. But the club president, Kylie, is mixing things up by inviting new members. And Lexi is in for a not-so-sweet surprise when she is cast in the school's production of *Romeo and Juliet*. If only she could be as confident onstage as she is in the kitchen. The icing on the cake: her secret crush is playing Romeo. Sounds like a recipe for trouble!

Can the girls' friendship stand the heat, or will the cupcake club go up in smoke?

Book
2

4/13

PUTTERHAM BRANCH
BROOKLINE PUBLIC LIBRARY
959 West Roxbury Parkway
Chestnut Hill, MA 02467

4/13